Praise for the Novel

"*Darok 9* is an exciting post-apocalyp[tic] on the harsh surface of the moon . . . [for] enthusiasts."–*The Midwest Book R[eview]*

"*Darok 9* has the excitement of a co[n] will love to see in the hands of their [...]

"*Darok 9* is a young adult book set i[...] page, the pace of the book is fast and always keeps the reader interested. Young adults will love the suspense that builds and builds as Hank and Will try to avoid being captured. . . I found that I hated to put this book down, as I really wanted to find out what was going to happen next. This is a fun book for not only young adults, but anyone who likes a good science fiction thriller." –**Conan Tigard,** *ReadingReview.com*

"*Darok 9* is another wonderful science fiction book for young adults by H.J. Ralles, author of *Keeper of the Kingdom*. Filled with nonstop action and suspense, it tells the story of a young scientist, Hank Havard, and his quest to keep his big discovery out of enemy hands. The [...] [found] are [...]ead [...]m [...]s us her [...] the [...]tion

[...]ok 9 [...] put and *Sci-*

Fi Source

"In the near future, Earth has been ravaged by ecological and military disaster. The few who survived have gone to our Moon, eking out an existence in domed towns called Daroks (Domed AtmospheRic Orbital Kommunities). Our plucky protagonist is a scientist researching ways to reduce the need for water by humans. Little does he know that treachery and betrayal lay all about him. An attack on the remote lab by the Fourth Quadrant sets him running from more than just falling masonry . . the double-crosses and double-double-crosses should be engaging for a young adult. –*Space Frontier Foundation, Moon Book of the Month Club*

D0230512

The Keeper Series

"Aimed at young adults, this is ingenious enough to appeal powerfully to adults who wonder how far this entire computer age can go. Ralles knows how to pace her story - the action moves in sharp chase-and-destroy scenes as Commanders hunt down the dangerous young boy. The characters are memorable, particularly the very human 101. And that ending . . . -is brilliant. A compelling read from exciting beginning to just as exciting ending." **–The Book Reader**

"*Keeper of the Kingdom* is a must read for children interested in computers and computer games. From the first page to the last there is no relief from the suspense and tension. H.J. Ralles has captivated anyone with a fascination for computer games, and has found a way to connect computer-literate children to reading." *–JoAn Martin, Review of Texas Books*

"Kids will be drawn into this timely sci-fi adventure about a boy who mysteriously becomes a character in his own computer game. The intriguing plot and growing suspense will hold their attention all the way through to the book's provocative ending." **–Carol Dengle,** *Dallas Public Library*

"This zoom-paced sci-fi adventure, set in the kingdom of Zaul, is a literary version of every kid's dream of a computer game. Keeper of the Kingdom may be touted for youngsters from 9 to 13, but I'll bet you my Spiderman ring that it will be a "sleeper" for adults as well." **–Johanna M. Brewer,** *Plano Star Courier*

"As in any good video game the PG-rated action is unrelenting, and the good guys never give up. *Keeper of the Kingdom* could be made easily into an adequate Nickelodeon-style kids' movie." *–VOYA*

"H.J. Ralles continues to offer readers a fascinating affiliation between computers and books. Her two 'Keeper' stories are wonderful reading experiences."*–The Baytown Sun*

"H.J. Ralles spins a wonderful Science Fiction tales aimed at younger readers, but has also created something that is quite enjoyable for book lovers of all ages." **–Conan Tigard,** *ReadingReview.com*

"Ralles knows how to turn out a first-rate story. And, how to make coming-of-age as suspenseful as nature makes it every day." **–Lisa DuMond,** *SFSite*

"*Keeper of the Empire* is a fun read, with action that grips you from the start. Excellent for middle school and reluctant readers; enjoyable and suspenseful." **–Christie Gibrich, Roanoake Public Library, Roanoke, Texas**

Darok 10

Darok 10

By

H.J. Ralles

Top Publications, Ltd.
Dallas, Texas

DAROK 10

A Top Publications Paperback

First Edition
12221 Merit Drive, Suite 950
Dallas, Texas 75251

ISBN#: 1-929976-31-3
Library of Congress 2004112644

Printed in the United States of America

For
Stephen and Rachel

Friendships come and go, but families are forever.
Kenny Rogers

Acknowledgments

As always, thanks to: Malcolm, Richard and Edward for your ideas and suggestions as well as your constant support; Brenda Quinn for her unprecedented editing, without which this book would not be what it is; Bill Manchee and all at Top Publications; my colleagues in the Plano Writers, the SCBWI and the NAWW, whose critiquing skills are exceptional and whose friendship means so much to me; and Motophoto, Plano, for great publicity photographs.

Chapter 1

Gunter Schumann gasped. His body stiffened.

The safe in the Cryolab was wide open and he hardly dared to venture inside. He felt sick and then hot. His fingers trembled as he unbuttoned the collar of his lab coat and stepped through the doorway. He fumbled for the light switch, catching his breath as the secure room was illuminated. Just as he had feared, box 15 had been forced open. Now he was *really* scared. Worse than that—he was terrified.

Gunter staggered forward, pulled out the metal box, and lifted the bent lid. He reached inside and ran his hand over the bottom, frantically feeling from corner to corner. But as he'd suspected, the box was empty.

His knees shook. "We're all doomed," he muttered. He closed the huge metal door of the safe and stumbled across the Cryolab toward the exit, trying to figure out what he should do next.

Gunter passed the three enormous cryotanks that dominated the room. Each contained fifteen human beings, frozen in fifteen clear cylinders that were arranged around the circumference. His eyes fell on tank 2. He shuddered. The patient preserved in cylinder 15 seemed to be looking at him through the glass. It was patient fifteen's safe box that had been forced open and emptied.

Panic gripped Gunter again. He hurriedly turned off the light and locked the Cryolab door behind him, only drawing breath when he heard the sound of the lock click into place.

In the bright hospital corridor, his discovery seemed less sinister. He wiped the perspiration from his balding head and stuffed the handkerchief back into the pocket of his lab coat. The elevator bell sounded. Gunter's heart raced again. He turned to see who would exit the elevator at the end of the corridor.

Will Conroy stepped out. Gunter relaxed slightly at the sight of his lab assistant's son but then wondered how he could get rid of him quickly. The fourteen-year-old was fascinated with the Cryolab and fancied himself as a leading cryonics scientist of the future. Although the Moon's current technology enabled people with certain conditions to be preserved at death, the technique for reviving them had not yet been perfected. Will wanted to be on the research team that made the breakthrough. He always had questions for Gunter . . . too many questions.

Will sauntered down the corridor toward him, hands shoved in his pant pockets and a wide grin fixed on his face. "Hi, Doc Schumann. How's things? Anybody get frozen this week?"

"No, not this week, Will," Gunter answered, praying that the boy wouldn't stop to chat with him. He smiled at him weakly, trying to hide his distress when all he could think about was box 15.

"I heard that our lunar scientists can now preserve heart attack victims."

"Look, I'm sorry, Will. I can't stop and talk tonight—I've got things I must do," said Gunter in a pleasant but curt manner.

"That's okay. We're going out to dinner with Uncle Hank and if I don't hurry Mom along we'll be late. Has she finished for the day?"

Gunter felt relieved that the boy was in a hurry. "Er...Rachel...yes...I think so. She was finishing up the lab records a few minutes ago." He could feel Will's eyes fixed on him.

Will's eyebrows raised inquiringly. "Are you feeling okay, Dr. Schumann?"

"Yes, just fine, thank you," Gunter replied. He scratched his beard and forced himself to widen his smile. When would the boy leave him to think in peace?

"Are you sure? You look rather pale," Will persisted.

"No, I'm fine, really. Nice of you to ask. I'm going straight home tonight. I'll be collecting my briefcase and plenty of weekend work when I've set the Cryolab alarm. Why don't you go and meet your mother?"

Will looked at him in a concerned way, seemed to hesitate and then continued along the corridor. Gunter sighed with relief as he watched the lanky youth disappear through the double doors of the Pathology Department. He turned back to face the Cryolab, and once again his frightening discovery consumed his thoughts. How had anyone got into the lab with all the security? He must get the system changed on Monday.

His mind raced. What should he do in the meantime? Until now he had kept the valuable contents of box 15 a secret. But this was an emergency. He would have to immediately contact Commander Richard Gillman and tell him what had been stolen. He stared at the alarm panel on the wall. Only he, the Commander and Rachel had an access code. How could a thief have got in? He started punching in the four-digit sequence to secure the Cryolab for the weekend.

Gunter heard movement. As he began to turn, searing pain shot through the side of his head. He yelled in agony and grabbed his ear. What was happening? He could barely see! Dizzy, he staggered sideways. He pressed his hands against the wall desperately trying to stay upright, but his knees buckled under him and he fell to the floor. It was too late. Someone knew about his connection to box 15.

* * * * *

Rachel pulled up the day's work on one of the Pathology Department computers. She hummed the Moon Net's latest hit as she saved the files and began to shut down the system for the night. Another week spent doing what she loved, although most people couldn't understand why her job was so important to her. It was hard explaining that working with dead bodies and testing blood samples was like putting together a jigsaw puzzle piece by piece. Maybe someday she'd discover a new viral strain or perhaps someday she'd save the lunar population from a killer disease. That was quite possible in the Daroks, where life was completely dependent upon generated oxygen and diseases spread rapidly.

Rachel looked at her watch. It was nearly six. Will barged through the double doors. She smiled at her son, who towered above her. "Great, you're just in time. Give me a hand to carry these folders into the office, and then I'm done for the day."

"And for the week," added Will.

"Yes, thank goodness for Fridays," said Rachel. "Put the folders on Dr. Schumann's desk. I can file them properly out back on Monday."

Will lifted the stack off the counter. "Uncle Hank decided to stay in the lobby," he said, walking into the small glass-fronted room. "He figured you'd hurry if you knew he was waiting!"

Rachel smiled. That was typical of her brother—always thinking of his stomach. Hank knew how she liked to chat as she cleared up for the night. She glanced at her watch again. "I thought Gunter would be back by now."

"I just saw Dr. Schumann outside the Cryolab," said Will. "He didn't look very well and he said he was going straight home."

"Really?" she scowled. "He seemed fine earlier and his briefcase is still here."

"He said he was taking a lot of weekend work with

him."

Rachel smiled. "That's Gunter. He's a workaholic. He never leaves here without another six hours of paperwork stuffed into his briefcase. I ought to wait for him and say goodnight."

"We'll be late, Mom, and I told him we were leaving right away."

Rachel shrugged. "Well then, I guess we can go. I just need to set the alarm on the rear elevator."

"Rear elevator?"

"It's used to bring down the dead from street level. Better than upsetting everyone by wheeling them through the hospital, don't you think?"

Will nodded and muttered, "I guess."

"It won't take a minute, I promise."

Will sighed. "Good, 'cause Uncle Hank made this dinner reservation months ago and we don't want to lose our table."

Rachel marched through the supply room and into a small lobby out back, aware that her son would soon be complaining about his rumbling stomach. The light on the panel was flashing, indicating that the alarm was already set. That was strange. She had signed for the last patient only two hours ago and she didn't remember setting the alarm. She and Gunter usually left the alarm off until the end of the day. She shrugged. Perhaps Gunter had already locked up for the night or maybe she was just getting forgetful.

Rachel returned to the office, removed her lab coat

and hung it on a hook by the door. "Okay, I'm done."

"Good. I'm starving!" replied Will, already on his way out the door.

The hospital basement seemed unusually quiet as Rachel led the way to the elevator. She shuddered as she passed the Cryolab. Her mind was working overtime, as always. That room and its contents made her uncomfortable.

"Mom, stop cringing! I don't get why you have such a dislike for cryonics."

"It's just a little creepy."

"Creepy? This is the future of science on the Moon—Uncle Hank will tell you! Imagine being able to freeze someone, revive them, cure the disease they died of, and give them a second chance to live! We're so close to being able to revive them, and I'm going to be part of the lunar team that does it!"

"Then you'd better put your mind to your studies," scolded Rachel. "How do you think your Uncle Hank got to be a renowned scientist? Not by playing computer games all day long, that's for sure."

She pressed the elevator button to go up to the lobby and caught a glimpse of herself in the mirrored doors. Her new shoulder-length haircut suited her, but right now it looked a mess. She reached for her handbag and her comb. "Darn, I forgot my bag. You carry on up and I'll be with you in a minute."

"Okay, but don't take too long. I'm starving!" Will stepped into the elevator and waved as the doors closed.

Just then Rachel heard a loud bang as if someone had slammed a door. She twisted quickly around and stared back down the corridor. Her stomach tightened. There was no one in sight.

She shook her head. She was being silly. *Pull yourself together and go and get your bag,* she thought, walking slowly toward the Pathology Department. Something made her stop in front of the Cryolab. It was as if some great force was preventing her from walking on. She pushed down on the door handle. The room was locked and nothing seemed out of the ordinary. The red light flashed on the alarm panel, as it should. This was crazy. What was she doing?

Rachel laughed and forced herself to continue toward her office. A splash of red on the carpet caught her eye. Its uneven shape was distinctly different from the pattern of the carpet, but the mark blended well with the crazy mixture of color. Perhaps the stain had always been there and she had never noticed it. She bent down and touched the spot with her index finger. Her heart quickened. It was wet.

She stared at the red on the tip of her finger. Blood—she was sure of it. She saw it every day. Fear engulfed her. She looked over her shoulder. Was someone watching her? Forget her purse—she had to get out of here. She wiped her fingertip on the carpet, raced back to the elevator and hammered on the button. Hours seemed to pass as she waited. The bell finally sounded. Rachel jumped inside and counted the seconds until the doors reopened in the hospital lobby.

She caught her breath and rushed over to where her brother and son sat waiting. The sight of them both, so alike and so happy, calmed her a little.

"Record time, Mom! It only took you four minutes!" said Will, getting to his feet.

Hank kissed her on the cheek, but then his face clouded. He put his hands on her shoulders and stepped back to look at her. "Rach, are you okay? You look like you've seen a ghost."

Rachel realized she was shaking. "It's probably nothing. I've just had a long day," she said, trying to put on a brave face.

"The Cryolab, right?" teased Will. He shook his hands in a ghost-like manner over his mother's head. "Mom works with dead bodies all day, every day, but she's scared that the ones who have been frozen will wake up and haunt her."

"Enough, Will," Hank reprimanded. "Seriously, Rach. Is something up?"

Will frowned. "Mom? Where's your bag? Didn't you go back and get it?"

Rachel gulped. "I never got that far. I...I...saw blood on the carpet in the corridor."

"Is that unusual?" asked Hank. "I mean, you work with blood samples, right?"

"But not on the carpet in the corridor, Hank!" she snapped. "Besides, the blood was wet!" Rachel stared at her fingertip, but there was no visible trace of blood to show them. "And it's not just that...I heard a door bang...but no one was there...and something felt different—almost like I was being watched."

"Slow down," said Hank, guiding her to one of the comfortable lobby chairs. "Now tell me everything again."

"There's nothing else to tell—that's just it. I didn't see anyone—just had this really bad feeling. I'm probably just being silly."

"But you get these feelings all the time, right, Mom?" said Will. "You know you hate the Cryolab. I watched you freak out just a minute ago. Come on, let's go eat, or we'll lose our table at the Lunar Café. You'll feel much better with some food in you."

"Just a minute, Will," said Hank. "Rach, did you see Dr. Schumann leave? Perhaps he was there and banged the door."

Rachel shook her head. "No, I didn't. And that's another thing that's strange. Will saw him in the corridor just a few minutes before I left. Gunter told him that he was going home in a minute. He'd set the Cryolab alarm as he always does, but I never passed him in the corridor going back for his briefcase. He *never* leaves without it...that and a load of work to do at home."

"Dr. Schumann *was* acting kind of weird," Will cut in. "I even asked him if he was feeling okay."

"Will, run and ask Jerry at the desk to check the sign-out register. See if Dr. Schumann has left the building," Hank said. "Oh, and get his VisionCom number so we can call him."

"I know I don't like the Cryolab," said Rachel, "but I pass the Cryonics Department every day and I *do not* 'freak out' as Will so nicely phrased it. I've never felt like this before!"

"I'm sure there's a reasonable explanation," replied Hank, patting his sister on the knee. "Perhaps it's because you're worried Dr. Schumann is ill."

Will returned and handed Hank a small card. "Here's Dr. Schumann's Com number, but he's still here, according to the register."

"Then why don't we all go and find him," Hank suggested. "You'll feel much better when you know he's okay."

"Yes, I think you're right." Rachel pulled herself out of the chair and exhaled heavily.

"I guess that means I've got to wait for dinner," mumbled Will.

Rachel sighed. "No matter how hungry you are, Will, it's not going to hurt you to wait for once. Besides, the reservation's for 6:30. We've got time yet."

"Growing boys think of their stomachs twenty-four hours a day," said Hank, as they descended in the elevator.

"That's because we're growing," retorted Will, "as you just pointed out."

Hank laughed. "Just make sure you don't follow in my footsteps and start growing out instead of up." He ruffled Will's blond hair.

Rachel grabbed Hank's hand as they left the elevator.

The corridor was empty. She led them into the Pathology Department. The lights were still on and Dr. Schumann's briefcase was still on the floor beside his desk. Her bag sat in plain sight on the countertop.

"Well, he's definitely not gone home," said Hank. "Where else might he be?"

Rachel shook her head. "Only the Cryolab. Since the hospital funding was cut, Gunter's been in charge of the Cryonics Department as well as Pathology. He was making his nightly check on the Cryolab when Will saw him."

"Perhaps he went back inside the Cryolab for something," suggested Hank.

Rachel nodded. "It's possible, I suppose. Though I can't think why. It's not as if there's anything to do in there except to make sure that the cryotanks are stable. All the cryonics research has been moved to the new labs in Darok 10. Besides, why would the alarm be set if Gunter had gone back inside?"

"Let's check out the Cryolab anyway and then we can go and get dinner," said Will.

Rachel picked up her bag and led the way back through the swinging doors. She punched her code into the keypad outside the Cryolab. The flashing red light turned green and a soft clunk sounded as the lock unbolted. She nervously pressed down on the handle but then hesitated.

"Don't worry, I'll go first, Mom," said Will, flicking on the lights as he entered. "See, there's nothing to be nervous about."

Hank and Will began walking around the room, their voices echoing under the high ceilings. Rachel hung by the door while they checked the laboratories out back. She looked around the room. With its white paneled walls and gray tiled floor, the Cryolab felt sterile and clinical. At the far end of the room, the huge steel door of the safe glinted in the light. In the center, three huge cylindrical cryotanks hummed quietly. Rachel turned away from the tank closest to her. She hated looking at the eerie faces of the patients with their fixed expressions. She preferred to think of them as patients and not as the dead—after all, they *were* waiting to be brought back to life.

"Everything seems fine," said Hank, as he and Will came back to the door.

Rachel nodded her agreement. She had to admit that the Cryolab was peaceful and that nothing seemed amiss.

Will draped his arm around her shoulders. "The doc's not here—unless he's in one of the tanks."

"Will!" Rachel scolded. "That's a really unpleasant thing to suggest!"

"Sorry, Mom, I couldn't resist." He shot her an impish smile.

Hank chuckled. "Let's go. There's nothing more to see here. Dr. Schumann has probably gone to another department." He took out the card that Will had given him. "We'll call his Com and see where he is."

"You can't. There's no reception down here." Rachel

closed the door to the Cryolab and reset the alarm.

"Okay, I'll call him later. Why don't you show me the blood stain?" Hank suggested.

She bent to the floor where she'd seen the spot just fifteen minutes before, but all she saw was the hexagonal pattern of the carpet. She ran her hand over the entire area trying to find the wet spot. "I...I don't see it now," she stammered.

"Are you sure this was the place, Mom?"

Rachel stood up and caught Will and Hank looking at each other. "I know what you're thinking. You're both thinking I've been working too hard, or that I'm seeing things because I hate the Cryolab."

"We didn't say that," said Hank.

"You don't have to. I can see it in your faces. The blood was here, I tell you! I saw it, and I felt it, and I'm not going mad!"

"Okay, okay," said Hank. "I believe you, but I just don't have an explanation."

Will sighed. "Can we *please* get dinner now?"

Rachel nodded and followed them to the elevator in silence. As the doors opened she turned and took one last look behind her. The light still shone in the Pathology Department waiting for the return of Gunter Schumann. She knew something was wrong, but exactly what, she had no idea.

Chapter 2

Hank chewed his last piece of chicken slowly, savoring the flavor and texture. He would pay dearly in ration points for tonight's dinner, but he had enjoyed every mouthful. It would be months before he could afford another piece of chicken at the Lunar Café, Darok 9's only restaurant. He'd had to book the table two months ago as there were only twenty small cloth-covered tables crammed into a tiny room. But the excellent food made the cramped conditions worth the wait and he wasn't about to rush through the experience.

"How's the chicken, Rach?" asked Hank, watching her push the same piece across her plate for the umpteenth time.

"Sorry, Hank. I know that you saved a long time for this meal, but I'm just not hungry."

Hank frowned. It was unlike his sister not to clean her plate, and she had hardly said a word all through dinner. The family often teased her about the Cryolab, but they all knew that she wasn't scared easily. He'd never seen her quite as shaken as she was tonight.

Hank handed his blue ration card to the waiter. Twenty valuable points would be deducted to cover the bill. He'd have to go easy for the next two weeks to make up for it.

They left the restaurant and walked down Armstrong Avenue. Hank looked up at the beautiful black sky and Will pointed out the various constellations. It was rare to be able to see the sky so clearly through the dome that protected the Darok. Often the dome was cloudy when the liquid crystal sandwiched between its silicon layers changed to combat the extreme lunar temperatures. Only for a short time each month was the dome clear enough to view the galaxy beyond.

Hank stared at the swirling clouds around the Earth. The blue planet looked inviting from where he stood, in spite of all the destruction that he knew existed on the surface. He drew in a deep breath. Pity the Darok air was manufactured and recycled. He had read articles about how air on Earth could smell damp or even scented by flowers. He had walked through the Darok 9 greenhouses, but was it the same? He imagined himself striding out of his home into fresh air or rain. How would it feel to have the wind on his cheeks? He shook his head. Generations of humans would never know.

Thankfully the Daroks' ventilation system had run without problems for decades and was closely guarded by the military. He knew that if the system ever malfunctioned, thousands would die within hours as the oxygen ran out. Would the military be able to evacuate everyone to another Darok in time to prevent a disaster?

He said goodnight to Rachel and Will at the corner of Sheppard Place and stood gazing at Earth for a few minutes more. He sighed. He wasn't ready to go home.

He was still bothered by Dr. Schumann's disappearance and he knew he wouldn't sleep until he found some explanation for his sister's strange behavior. When he was sure that Will and Rachel were out of sight, he walked away from his apartment and doubled back down Armstrong Avenue toward the hospital.

He decided he'd call his old friend, Mac Stewart, a forensics expert for the Darok 9 security force. Hank flipped open his brand new VisionCom and wondered how he had managed so long without this wonderful piece of technology. He punched in Mac's number and seconds later Mac's ruddy face and mass of red hair appeared on the tiny two-inch screen.

"Sorry to bother you so late," said Hank, "but I need a big favor—tonight if possible."

"Not much of tonight left," Mac grumbled. "I've just got ready for bed."

"Could you throw on some clothes, bring your kit and meet me in the hospital lobby? It's really important."

Mac grinned. "I'll be there in five minutes, but it'll cost you."

"Thanks, Mac...I appreciate it."

Hank closed the VisionCom and crossed into Gemini Court. He headed toward the hospital, which dominated the end of the street. It was Darok 9's architectural showcase with its illuminated entrance and ostentatious fountains. He stopped briefly to watch the cascading water. Even after his discovery of SH33, a wonder drug that had helped to relieve the water shortage in the First

Quadrant, fountains like these were rare in any of the ten Daroks.

Hank shuffled through the revolving hospital doors, walked up to the front desk, and checked the register on the monitor. It was now 9:50 p.m. and Dr. Schumann still hadn't signed out. Hank was puzzled. Who would Schumann visit in the building at this time of night?

"Hey there, what's so urgent?"

Hank turned around. The tall lean frame of his old college friend towered over him. "Hi, Mac. Thanks for coming at such short notice, especially on a Friday night. We need to go down to the Cryonics Department. I'll explain in the elevator."

Mac grinned. "You'll owe me for this, big time." He clutched his heavy forensics bag in both hands.

Hank waited for the elevator doors to close to make sure that their conversation wasn't overheard. "I need you to test the carpet outside the Cryolab."

Mac's face creased. "What am I testing for, exactly?"

"Traces of blood."

"Now you've got me interested," said Mac. "Where there's blood there's a case to be solved."

"There may not be." The doors reopened and Hank stepped into the basement corridor. "I just need to know."

"Need to know what?"

Hank shook his head. "I'll tell you later. Let's just see what you find first." He squatted down where Rachel had claimed she had seen blood. "Can you test an area about four square feet?"

"No problem," replied Mac. He opened his case and took out swabs and a small vial of clear liquid.

Hank leaned against the wall opposite the Cryolab and watched his friend work. He trusted Mac completely and knew he'd keep this quiet.

After a few minutes, Hank's eyes wandered to the door to the Cryolab. What had spooked Rachel? His eyes followed a line down the wall from the flashing alarm to the floor. Something caught his attention on the baseboard next to the door. He stepped across the corridor. Was that a speck of red? "Test the wall as well, can you?"

Mac glanced sideways. "Sure."

"Find anything?" asked Hank when Mac pulled off his rubber gloves a few minutes later.

Mac nodded. "There's definitely traces of blood on both the carpet and the baseboard. It's type O negative. I'll tell you what—I'll treat this as an investigation and run a full DNA test tomorrow morning."

"So, Rachel *was* right," muttered Hank.

"Right about what?" asked Mac, as he put away his equipment and the samples he'd collected. "Don't leave a guy in suspense—you've got to fill me in!"

Hank propped himself against the wall. He sighed. "It's all very strange. There's not a lot to go on and there may be nothing to worry about. I don't want to set off alarm bells needlessly."

Mac frowned. "Come on, Hank. I've known you a long time. Your hunches are often right. What's bugging you?"

"We can't find Dr. Schumann. It's only been a few hours and he's probably still in the building—but something just isn't quite right. Rachel thought she was being watched when she was leaving tonight. She also swore that she found fresh blood on this carpet. But when she came to show Will and me, no more than fifteen minutes later, the blood had disappeared."

Mac grinned. "Wanna see what else I found?" His eyes sparkled knowingly.

"What? Tell me."

"Exhibit A," said Mac, holding up a small clear container. "Short red hair—and not mine. And it gets better...I also detected a cleaning agent on the carpet."

"A cleaning agent?" questioned Hank.

Mac nodded. "It's quite possible that someone *was* in one of these rooms watching Rachel, and when she left to get you, that person cleaned the carpet with a quick-drying cleaning solution. The cleaning agent I found was fresh and only on a small area of the carpet, so we're *not* talking about something that would be used during the monthly hospital carpet cleaning."

Hank bit his lip. "What have we stumbled on here?"

"That's for you and the Darok 9 security force to determine." Mac clipped his case together.

"Do me a favor, Mac. Will you sit on this information for twenty-four hours? I want to talk to Rachel and locate Dr. Schumann before word of this gets out. He may have a perfectly logical explanation."

Mac nodded. "Yeah, yeah, I thought as much. You don't want to look like an idiot. Just remember—you owe me big time," he said, pointing his finger.

"Just let me know when you need a return favor. I'm going to stay here and see if I can find Dr. Schumann."

"Keep me updated," said Mac. "And Hank, stay out of trouble. You're a scientist, not a member of the security force. If I don't hear from you by tomorrow night, I'm taking this information straight to the top. Richard Gillman will be very interested—even on a Sunday."

Hank nodded. "Thanks, mate."

He watched Mac leave and then returned to the Pathology Department. The lights were still on and Schumann's briefcase still stood beside the desk. Hank lifted the briefcase on top of the desk and unfastened the metal locks at either end. By the jumble of creased papers inside, Hank guessed that either someone had searched through the case, or Schumann had hastily packed it. Hank looked at the open filing cabinet, the floor scattered with folders, and then the memory cards strewn across the desk. He knew from Rachel's tales of her work with Dr. Schumann that he was a meticulous man. Hank felt sure he wouldn't have created such a mess. Had someone broken into Schumann's office?

Hank gathered up the files from the floor and the memory cards from the desk. Perhaps they were the key to the mysterious events of the evening. He put them into the case and closed the lid. It was then that he noticed Gunter Schumann's hand-held VisionCom lying on the desk. Hank fingered it uneasily. So much for reaching Schumann on his Com. What he had already learned from Mac was disturbing, but now his mind was whirling with questions and fears. Hank picked up the case and turned off the lamp.

The hospital VisionCom on Schumann's desk rang. Hank jumped. He turned back to the desk, and fumbled in the dark for the lamp switch. He stared down at the Com screen. Should he answer it? His hand hesitated over the accept button. Then slowly he pushed it.

The screen displayed the words *PICTURE TRANSMISSION BLOCKED*. The caller coughed loudly and then cleared his throat. "Mr. Havard, you've been busy tonight. Keep your nose out of what doesn't concern you—if you value your family and friends." The line went dead.

Hank sat stunned for a few seconds and then turned off the Com. He felt suddenly cold. Someone had been watching him. Worse still, that someone knew his name.

Chapter 3

Hank approached Kennedy Plaza, his stomach in knots. He had detoured through the Darok 9 streets and skulked up and down the alleyways for thirty minutes. He clutched Gunter's black briefcase to his chest. Whoever had been watching him earlier might still be following him. The last thing he wanted was to put Rachel and her family in danger.

He'd been through every department at the hospital and no one had seen Gunter Schumann. There'd been no answer at his apartment on Canaveral Street and the concierge in the complex hadn't seen Dr. Schumann since he'd left for the hospital at seven this morning. He didn't know how he would break the bad news to Rachel.

When he was sure that no one had tailed him, Hank darted across the plaza and up to the Conroys' front door. He drew in a deep breath, and looked over his shoulder as he knocked gently.

Will opened the door. His welcoming expression turned quickly to anxiety. He looked at his watch. "Hi, Uncle Hank. Is something wrong?"

Hank pushed past Will and closed the front door quickly behind him. "I know...it's nearly midnight. I'm sorry to come around so late. Don't suppose your mom's still up?"

Will shook his head and yawned. "You've got to be kidding. She went to bed long ago. I was just playing my new computer game."

"Ah," said Hank. "It's pretty late for that, isn't it?"

"It's the school holidays. I can sleep in tomorrow."

"Don't wake your mom. Let her sleep—she was so upset this evening. I can talk to her in the morning. When does your dad get back from Darok 10?"

"At the end of next week."

"Oh," said Hank, his spirits falling. Who else he could trust?

"Wanna tell me what you found out?"

Hank smiled. "You're too sharp for your own good. Your mother will be livid if I get you involved."

"Is that Dr. Schumann's briefcase?"

Hank hesitated and then nodded. Why not confide in his nephew—he was fourteen and a smart kid. He wanted to run his ideas by someone, and he enjoyed working with Will. "Okay, I'll show you what I've found. How can I refuse a future scientist's curiosity? Let's see what you make of the situation."

Will's face lit up. He grabbed the tin of cookies from the kitchen table and led Hank into the study, quietly closing the door behind them.

Hank set Schumann's briefcase next to the computer on the desk and opened it.

"He's not very organized," said Will, looking at the mess of files and loose papers.

"I put the files in there. Most of them were thrown

across the floor. It looked as though someone had been through the doc's office looking for something."

For several moments Will seemed stunned as he took in Hank's words. "You think?"

"Almost certain," muttered Hank.

"So you believe Mom was right all along and that something's happened to Dr. Schumann?"

"It's beginning to look that way," said Hank. "No one has seen Dr. Schumann and there *was* blood on the carpet."

Will's eyes widened. "No kidding! How did you find that out?"

"You know Mac Stewart, my friend that works in forensics?"

Will nodded. "I've met him a couple of times."

"I called him after dinner. He tested the carpet outside the lab an hour ago," said Hank, picking up the first file.

"Then how did the blood disappear so fast?"

"Someone used a quick-drying cleaning solution to remove it after your mother was there and before we arrived."

Will slumped in his computer chair. "Now I feel really bad about teasing Mom. I don't know what I thought, but I didn't really believe her."

Hank shook his head. "Don't worry, you're not the only one. Something's not right and I want to get to the bottom of it." Hank decided he'd said enough. There was no sense in telling Will about the threatening Com call and worrying him unnecessarily. He opened up the first file. "Let's see what we have here. I'll take the folders and you take the memory cards. There are half a dozen in the case. Bring up the contents on the optical computer and see what you can find."

"Pull up a comfy chair," said Will. He motioned to a metal monstrosity with a padded seat in the corner of the room.

Hank dragged the chair up to the desk and began to sort through the papers. He smiled to himself. Comfy and paper—two words that had no real meaning on the Moon. He wondered what a really comfortable chair might feel like. Rachel had used 500 precious points from her red ration card for this ugly metal chair with a cushion. As for paper—what he called paper was actually a synthetic equivalent. With no trees, and a limited supply of wood brought from Earth, there was no real paper. If computer records weren't adequate, a manufactured synthetic paper was used, but it didn't have the soothing feel of the real samples of paper that he'd once felt in the Darok 9 museum.

Hank watched as Will pushed a memory card into the slot under the huge monitor, then picked up the cushioned headset and adjusted the tiny microphone. "Search files on cards one and two," he instructed the computer and turned to Hank. "What exactly are we looking for?"

"Wish I knew. Anything that strikes you as odd or unusual...records that don't match...I guess I'm looking for a reason why someone might be interested in the doctor and his work."

As Will continued on the computer, Hank turned his attention back to the manila folders. They seemed to be a random mixture of names and subjects. The first one he picked up contained pathology lab results for the week. Hank studied each sheet. There were no cases of unusual diseases and nothing sinister about any report.

"All pathology reports are normal," Hank mumbled, putting them back into the folder.

"This memory card seems to have similar information," said Will, scanning the contents of the file. "You should check these records against the ones you have—these numbers mean nothing to me. I'm no scientist." Will smiled. "Yet."

Hank laughed. "One day you'll be explaining formulae to me." He picked up another file, which contained a dozen records of autopsies performed by the new bodyscan machine. Hank browsed through the paperwork. Nothing seemed unusual. He yawned, put the files down, and picked a cookie out of the tin. As he took his first bite, he noticed a dark brown folder sticking out from the pile of cream-colored folders. He pulled it to the top. On the front was a yellow label with 'M.J. Rigby' printed in black ink. Hank flipped it open. It was empty. He stared at the blank inside and then at the pile of crumpled papers that he had found stuffed in Schumann's briefcase. With the cookie clenched between his teeth, Hank rifled through the loose sheets. None matched the name on the folder.

"Odd," muttered Hank.

"What have you found?" asked Will.

"Probably nothing. Have you got this week's body scans on memory card?"

Will picked up a card marked 'B&T body scans' and replaced the other. "This it?"

Hank peered at the screen and nodded. "B&T stands for bone and tissue. Have you got M.J. Rigby listed?"

Will scrolled down the alphabetized list and shook his head. "No such name."

"Now go back to the memory card for blood tests. See if M.J. Rigby is listed."

Will switched cards. "No, the name doesn't appear anywhere."

"I wonder who he was?" said Hank. "I've got more files with names on here," said Hank picking up a pile from the desk. "Let's check off the files with the names you have listed on both cards."

Hank went through each file, reading the name of every person. All other records matched. He flipped the empty brown folder against the desk in frustration. "None of the others are empty. I probably dropped the information in my rush to leave the hospital."

"Then why isn't the name in the computer records either?"

Hank sighed. "Good point. It may have been lost before your mom had a chance to add the record to the data base. I'm sure there are discrepancies like this all the time. That's why we still keep written files in spite of computer technology.   It's always good to have a backup."

"Mom's got a good memory.   She'll remember the name."

"Well, it's now 2 a.m.," said Hank, looking at his watch. "That's enough for one night.   Time for bed."

Will levered himself out of the swivel chair. "Are you coming back in the morning?"

"I've got a couple of things I want to check up on first. Do me a favor—have another look through the files in the morning.   See if there are any other names that don't appear in both Schumann's files and the memory cards."

"No problem.   I'm one week into my school vacation and I'm bored already.   Mom will be relieved I'm doing something other than playing computer games."

Hank smiled. "I'm not sure she'll be too pleased about this!   But you might want to ask her about M.J. Rigby."

"Sure thing, Uncle Hank."

"I'll go out the back door," said Hank, heading through the kitchen.   "It's quicker."

"Is it?"   Will looked really perplexed.   "Could have fooled me. I always thought that..."

Hank winked.   "Try it some time."

Will gave him a confused look and Hank decided he'd say no more. If anyone had seen him go in the front door of Will's house he hoped they'd still be watching the front door for him to leave.   He patted Will on the shoulder, looked both ways and stepped into the dimly lit back alley.

Hank walked past the huge recycling containers and turned the corner into another alley, the only light glimmering from the main street in the distance. He heard a rustle and his back prickled. Was someone there? As he looked up, a masked figure in black leaped from one of the fire escapes, landing directly in his path. He gasped and instinctively stepped backward, his heart pounding. The figure lunged and pressed something sharp into his chest. Fearing that it was a weapon, he quickly raised his hands above his head.

The shadowy figure cleared his throat. "You don't listen too well, Mr. Havard." The voice was scratchy and strained.

Hank tried to remain calm, but his stomach churned. He peered into the darkness trying to make out the identity of his attacker. The face and hair were completely obscured by a ski mask, but those penetrating eyes, glinting in the half-light, had a look that he had seen before. And it was the same voice that he'd heard on the VisionCom earlier. It was neither deep nor high-pitched, but distinctive and somehow familiar. Who was this? In the dark of the alleyway, he could barely make out the build of the figure in black. From the angle of the weapon, though, he worked out that the man was much shorter than himself.

"This is your final warning, Mr. Havard. Stay out of what doesn't concern you."

Hank's heart raced. "What have you done with Gunter Schumann?"

"*That* doesn't concern you!" the attacker snarled. "Now get walking and keep walking. Keep your mouth shut or it will be shut for you!"

Hank decided he'd pushed his luck far enough. It was time to do as he was told. Even though his knees felt like jelly, he brushed past his attacker and strode quickly toward Armstrong Avenue. He braced himself, half expecting to be shot in the back. Every step seemed to take forever. He counted his footsteps, focusing on the main street ahead.

After the longest walk of his life, he reached the end of the alley and the safety of the powerful overhead lights. Still shaking, he finally dared to look back. The alley was empty and his attacker had disappeared. Now what should he do? Were Will and Rachel in any danger?

* * * * *

Will returned to the study to switch off the computer for the night. He collected the tiny memory cards and was about to put them back into the briefcase when he stopped. Something told him to make copies. He had learned last year, after his uncle's research was stolen, that copies were very useful things.

Will ferreted in the desk drawer for some blank cards and inserted them one at a time into the optical computer. He quickly made copies of each. Where would be a safe place to hide them?

He shut down the computer and slipped the originals

back inside the zippered pocket in the briefcase lid. His fingertips brushed against something cold. Curious, he shoved his fingers into the bottom corner of the zippered pocket and felt a small metallic object. He couldn't get his whole hand inside the tight opening to retrieve it. With his fingertips he worked the object carefully up to the top and pulled out a tiny brass key on a thin red ribbon. Puzzled by its shape and size, he turned it over in his hand. It was dull and tarnished, too small to be a door key and too thick for a desk or filing cabinet. He dropped it into his pocket along with the copies of Schumann's memory cards, and turned out the light.

Will crept down the hallway to his bedroom, careful not to wake his mother. He stripped off his clothes, dropped them on the floor by the side of his bed, and crawled under the covers.

Sleep did not come easily. His mind was working overtime. In the morning his first job would be to hide the memory cards, and his second, to find out what the key opened. Will looked at his clock. The red numbers glowed 2:25.

He tossed and turned for another twenty minutes, ending up on his side facing the bedroom door. A glimmer of light shone underneath. Will sat up in bed. Hadn't it been dark a moment ago? Hadn't he turned off the study light? Yes, he distinctly remembered doing so. The light was too faint to be coming from the hallway. It had to be the study lamp.

Could it be his mother? Without a sound he turned

back his covers, stepped quietly on to the tiled floor, and tiptoed to the door. Slowly he turned the handle and opened it a crack. His mother's door was firmly shut and the light still out, but he heard papers rustling.

Will's pulse quickened. He could see a long shadow on the hallway wall opposite the study. Someone was standing beside the desk. Will stood behind the door with his back against the wall, heart pounding, desperately hoping that the intruder would leave. His legs ached. He breathed deeply, trying to calm his nerves. What should he do? If he confronted the intruder, he might put his life, and his mother's life, at risk. Staying put seemed the best idea.

There was a light tap on the front door. Will swallowed hard. Had Uncle Hank returned? Should he answer the door? If he showed himself would the intruder run or defend himself? Options raced through Will's mind but he remained fixed to the spot behind his bedroom door. Nothing he could think of seemed the right thing to do.

The light in the study went out. Will listened in the darkness for approaching footsteps, but there were none. Was that the sound of the back door opening? Heart still pounding, he crawled over to his window and carefully lifted the curtain. A thin figure was running down the alley away from his home.

There was another tap on the front door. Will tiptoed down the corridor in the dark. He peered through the peephole and sighed with relief when he saw his uncle standing outside. He quickly let him in.

"Am I ever pleased to see you!" said Will, hugging his Uncle Hank.

"What happened?" Hank whispered.

"Someone broke in."

"Are you okay?"

Will nodded. "They were in the study. I didn't know what to do so I stayed in my bedroom. Mom slept through the whole thing."

"Probably good that she did," replied Hank. "I'm glad I came back."

"Why did you?"

"Someone threatened me in the alley."

"No kidding! Are you okay?"

"Yeah, fine thanks. So, let's take a look in the study and see what they took."

Will turned on the table lamp. He gasped. The briefcase was still sitting on the desk by the computer, but Schumann's files were scattered all over the carpet. "Looks as though somebody wanted something from the doc's files."

"But what?" said Hank. "We've already looked at them and found nothing out of the ordinary. We'll look again tomorrow. I guess we'd better clean up this mess."

"Don't worry, I'll do it in the morning. It's late—or should I say early." Will yawned. "I've got to get some sleep and I don't want to wake Mom."

"You're right. I'll be back first thing. Knowing your mom, she's going to be upset when she hears about this. Keep the VisionCom by your bed and call the security force if you hear *anything* that worries you!"

"Will do, Uncle Hank."

"I doubt if the intruder will be back tonight," said Hank, looking around before stepping into the plaza.

Will closed the front door and then checked the lock on the kitchen door, returning to the study to turn off the lamp on his way back to bed. He stared at the folders strewn across the floor. It was no good—he had to clean up Schumann's files before his mom got up. She was already stressed, and if she saw the mess before he had a chance to explain, she'd freak out.

He picked up the first file and then with a jolt remembered the memory cards. He leaned over the desk and anxiously reached inside the briefcase pocket. The memory cards were gone. What was on those cards that the intruder could have wanted? He finished gathering up the papers, pleased that he'd thought to make copies of the memory cards an hour earlier. He collected the files and placed them back on the desk in a neat pile. Then it struck him. The brown folder marked M.J. Rigby was also missing.

Chapter 4

Will recounted the events of the night before to his mother. Her mouth gaped as she leaned against the kitchen sink listening to him.

"And you didn't think to wake me?" she shouted. "I can't believe I slept through all of this! You should have called Darok 9 security force immediately! There might have been fingerprints. By cleaning up you've compromised any investigation there could have been."

Will sighed as he sat down at the kitchen table. He hoped Uncle Hank was on his way over to help calm his mother. He felt the key in his pocket. "Mom, it wasn't a normal burglary, don't you see? It's all connected with Dr. Schumann. The intruder took nothing but the Pathology Department memory cards."

"What could Gunter have known that someone would want so desperately? I'm so worried about him."

"Maybe it has something to do with M.J. Rigby," said Will.

Rachel frowned. "Who's M.J. Rigby?"

"I was hoping you could tell us," said Hank, coming through the kitchen door. "M.J. Rigby was written on one of the folders but there was nothing in the folder and no computer record of that person." He turned to Will. "How are you doing this morning?"

"You knew about this, Hank?" screamed Rachel.

Hank nodded. "I had a similar encounter in the alleyway and came back to check on you both."

"What do you mean, a similar encounter?" she screeched. "Are you okay?"

"Sure," said Hank casually. "Just someone trying to scare me off with threats. I went home, waited ten minutes, and then doubled back. I must have scared off the intruder when I knocked on your door."

"I can't believe that neither of you thought to wake me!"

Hank put his arm around Rachel. "We did think about it...but you needed your sleep. Besides, it was over and there was nothing you could have done at three in the morning."

"I don't get it," said his mother, finally sitting down at the table. "We don't do any top secret work in the hospital labs. Any Darok 9 resident can get access to those records."

"And you don't know who M.J. Rigby is?" asked Will a second time.

She shook her head. "Never heard the name before. We certainly haven't done blood tests or body scans on anyone by that name recently. I know I'd remember because we do so few in a month."

"That file folder was also taken," Will added.

Hank raised his eyebrows. "Was it?"

"But it was empty to begin with," said Will. "So what use is that to anyone?"

"Someone who doesn't want us to remember the name," replied Hank. "Shame we've lost the memory cards. I'll have to think of a new approach."

Will dug deep in his pockets and laid the copies of the memory cards out on the table in a long line. "I learned my lesson last year when your research was stolen," he said with a smile.

Hank beamed. "Fantastic! You'll make a detective as well as a scientist. I can see by your smug expression that you're proud of yourself, and you should be."

Will laughed and dipped into his pocket again. "But the best is yet to come!" He pulled out the little brass key, slipped the ribbon over his index finger and dangled it in front of his uncle's face. "I also found this in the briefcase."

Hank reached forward and lifted the key off Will's finger. "Rach, any idea what this might belong to?"

She shook her head. "Never seen it before. It's not a key to anything in the Pathology Department."

"What about the Cryolab?" Hank asked.

She shook her head again. "No, don't think so. The boxes in the Cryolab safe all have digital combination locks."

"Then we start with Schumann's apartment," said Hank.

Rachel gasped. "You're not serious, Hank! Just when are you going to inform the security force?"

"In about twelve hours," replied Hank. "If Schumann's life is in danger, the fewer people that know about this the better. It's quite possible that someone on the security force is involved."

"Oh, Hank," Rachel sighed. "You and your espionage theories. Just because you work on top secret military projects doesn't mean that you should be suspicious of everyone around you—especially those in Darok 9 who protect us. You've got to learn to trust people."

"I do, but only those close to me. My friend Mac, who did the forensic work last night, will share what he found with Richard Gillman, head of the Darok 9 security force, tomorrow morning. If Schumann doesn't turn up for work on Monday, the hospital will call Gillman anyway. Just give me today, Rach. It's Saturday—I've no work to do. Let's see what we can find out."

"And what about the risk? You've already been threatened once and my home has been broken into. Isn't that enough?"

Will could sit back no longer listening to them argue. He loved the thrill of detective work with Uncle Hank. His boring school holidays had suddenly become exciting and his mother was threatening to stop his fun. "We weren't in any danger, Mom. Whoever broke in here last night only wanted Doc Schumann's records."

"I can see you're on your uncle's side," said his mother, "but that's very naïve. How do you know you weren't in any danger or that the attacker won't be back? Gunter's already missing, and who knows what has happened to him, and your uncle was threatened in the alleyway. If you keep investigating, *you* might be the next one to disappear."

"Come on, Mom," Will pleaded. He got up and put his arms around his mother. He could always soften her up with a hug. "Just give Uncle Hank today. He's got to leave for Darok 10 tomorrow morning anyway."

Hank's face dropped. "Heck, I'd forgotten about that. I'm due to start my new research project next week in the new Darok 10 labs. I haven't even packed yet."

"Nine hours . . . and no more," said his mother with a stern expression. "I'll give you until six tonight. If Gunter's not been found by then, I'll call Richard Gillman myself—and I don't care that it's the weekend!"

Will kissed his mom on the cheek. "Thanks, Mom. We'll find Dr. Schumann. You won't be sorry."

"I already am," she moaned.

"So, where do we begin?" Will asked his uncle eagerly.

"I want you to take the copies of the memory cards and visit your friend Maddie," said Hank. "She's great with computer programs and knows her way around the Moon Net better than anyone in Darok 9. See what she can find out about M.J. Rigby."

Will grabbed the memory cards from the table. "I'm on my way. What are you guys going to do?"

Hank grinned at Rachel. "I was hoping your mother would come with me to Dr. Schumann's apartment. She's good at talking her way into places."

Rachel scowled. "I can see I'm not going to be able to stay out of this."

"You got us into it," Hank teased. "If you speak to the

concierge nicely we might get lucky and get past the front desk without having to climb the fire escape."

Rachel sighed heavily. "I can't believe I'm agreeing to this."

Will laughed. "I can!"

* * * * *

Hank turned the corner of Armstrong Avenue with Rachel and headed toward Gunter Schumann's fancy apartment complex near the hospital. Hank wondered why anyone would pay the exorbitant rent for such a place, but then, what else was there to spend your money on in Darok 9? *Food*, thought Hank. *I'd rather go to the Lunar Café once a month.*

Hank stopped dead in the center of Canaveral Street. Parked outside the Starlight Apartments was a sobering sight—a Darok 9 titanium-powered ambulance. There were only seven vehicles in Darok 9 and it was rare to see any of them on the narrow cobbled streets. Three belonged to Emergency Services, two were Public Health trucks, and two made deliveries from the factories.

A small crowd had gathered around the silver vehicle, its flashing red lights drawing Darok 9 residents to the scene. Hank approached just as the medics closed the two rear doors.

"Do you...do you think...they've found Gunter?" stammered Rachel. "I hope he's okay."

"Let's find out." Hank approached a short woman at

the back of the crowd. "Excuse me, Madam. Do you know who's in the ambulance?"

"The man in 4C. He took an overdose," she delighted in recounting, "but they think he'll be okay."

"4C?" questioned Rachel.

The woman nodded and continued talking to the man next to her.

"That's not Gunter," said Rachel, showing obvious relief. "He's in 2J, thank goodness."

Hank's stomach churned. "No, it's not Gunter. It's my friend, Mac." He looked up at the façade of the apartment complex not wanting to believe it.

"Oh, Hank! I'm so sorry!" gasped Rachel, covering her open mouth with her hand.

Hank stumbled over to one of the iron benches on the sidewalk. He lowered himself carefully onto the seat, trying to absorb the news. "Mac...why Mac? He wouldn't...he was opposed to any kind of drugs. The man never took so much as a cough drop."

Rachel sat down next to Hank and wrapped her arm around his slumped shoulders. "You don't think it's got anything to do with..."

"Gunter Schumann?" finished Hank. He boiled with rage. "I'd bet my life on it. Whoever warned me off last night and broke into your apartment also visited Mac. This morning Mac was going to do a DNA test on the blood sample he found on the carpet."

"So you think someone was trying to prevent Mac from doing the test," said Rachel.

"Looks like they succeeded," replied Hank bitterly. "I'll bet the samples he gathered have now disappeared. But how did they find out that Mac even had the samples? I know he wouldn't have told anyone else."

"You're scaring me, Hank," said Rachel. "You're suddenly saying '*they*' like we're not looking for one person in Darok 9."

"Or any of the other Daroks," added Hank.

"What?" whispered Rachel. "You think there's an outside connection and that we're up against the governments in the other Quadrants?"

"It's happened before. Ever since the other three Lunar Quadrants united, I've been waiting for further attacks on First Quadrant Daroks."

"But this is *not* an attack," said Rachel indignantly. "All we have is Gunter's disappearance."

"...*and* threats *and* an attempt on Mac's life. Attacks on the Daroks can come in many shapes and forms. I'm beginning to think that maybe Gunter Schumann knew something of real importance. Perhaps something of value to the United Quadrants. I've just got to figure out what and who's involved. I'll go and see Gillman tonight."

Rachel nodded her approval. "I'm relieved. It doesn't matter if it's just someone with a grievance against Gunter or something more sinister, the security force should be dealing with it—not you and Will."

Hank watched the ambulance drive away. The crowd dispersed and the residents of the Starlight Apartments began to walk back up the steps.

"Let's go," said Hank, still somewhat dazed. "If we join the crowd we can get past the front desk and up to Gunter's apartment without being questioned. With all these people the concierge won't notice us."

"How will we get inside his apartment?" whispered Rachel. "Don't forget this place has coded doors, not traditional locks."

"Yeah, that's one of the features of the Starlight that costs residents extra ration coupons—but it obviously didn't protect Mac," mused Hank. He patted his pocket. "Don't worry. I've got a decoder."

"A what?"

"You'll see. Don't forget I have military clearance. I can get my hands on all kinds of neat little gadgets."

Hank walked beside a tall man as they crossed the lobby, hoping the man would shield him from the concierge.

"Mr. Havard. How can I help you?" boomed the concierge above the chatter.

Hank flushed with embarrassment as he turned to face the concierge he'd questioned about Gunter Schumann just twelve hours before. He watched Rachel continue to the elevator unnoticed.

"I'm visiting Dr. Schumann," replied Hank.

The concierge was a huge man with eyebrows that met in the middle. He scowled at Hank. "You found him, then? I'm pleased. You had me worried when you dropped by last night."

"We're all relieved," said Hank, trying to sound casual.

"Gunter called me at home. I've got to collect some files."

"I'll have to buzz his apartment and check he's in."

"He is," said an elderly woman waiting for the elevator. "I saw him go into his apartment less than an hour ago."

"Thank you, Mrs. Harrington." The concierge eyed Hank with suspicion and then nodded. "Okay, you can sign the register. You know the procedure for visiting Starlight residents, Mr. Havard. Next time, if you don't stop at the desk, I'll be obliged to call the security force to escort you out of the building."

Hank grinned sheepishly. The thought of being surrounded by clones and marched onto the street did not appeal to him. He scrawled his name on the desktop monitor and held his thumb up to the fingerprint scanner.

"*Do* call and see me on your way out," the concierge said with a hint of sarcasm.

Hank saluted him, military style, and made a beeline for the elevator. He squeezed between the closing doors. Rachel was inside, squashed between two burly men. She gave him a wry smile. They rose in silence to the second floor. Hank stepped out and waited for Rachel to exit.

"That wasn't any fun," she said, straightening her hair. "I could hardly breathe in there."

"It was a bit claustrophobic," said Hank, reading the door numbers as he walked along. He stopped outside 2J. "This is it."

Rachel drew in a deep breath and knocked. She waited a minute and then looked at Hank with her '*what now?'* expression that he knew so well.

"Try knocking again—but loudly this time," suggested Hank.

Rachel hammered heavily on the door. There was still no reply. She shrugged. "Guess the old lady was wrong."

"Perhaps not."

"How do you mean?"

"Her sight is probably failing," replied Hank. He lowered his voice. "I suspect that she saw someone entering the apartment, but it wasn't Gunter. There's only one thing left to do." He removed the decoder from his pocket and pushed the pointed end into a small metallic slot on the bottom of the keypad. "I know it's against the law, and I wouldn't normally break into someone's home, but since we're trying to help Gunter, I feel justified." Within seconds the keypad beeped four times and the word ENTER flashed on a small screen next to the door.

Hank passed the decoder to Rachel to hold. He pressed down on the handle with his left hand. The door clicked and swung open on its own.

"Clever," said Rachel.

Hank hesitated on the threshold, listening for sounds of an intruder. It seemed safe to enter. He ushered Rachel through the tiny foyer into the main living area, then stopped in his tracks. The apartment had been ripped apart. Chairs had been upturned, pictures pulled off the walls, and all of Gunter's photographs and ornaments cleared off the shelves and tossed into the middle of the room. Hank stared in horror at the mess.

Rachel seemed to be glued to one spot as she surveyed the damage. "I've never seen anything like it."

Hank shook his head and stepped over clothing, piles of papers and overturned furniture. "Whoever did this was pretty thorough."

"What could they have been looking for, Hank?"

"Now *you're* saying 'they'. If we knew what they wanted, we'd already have it. But it's definitely something small."

"Why do you say that?" asked Rachel.

"Well, if you're searching for something big then you don't bother looking for it in a small place. Everything in this room has been trashed. Even the pictures have been taken off the walls." Hank picked up a few books and placed them back on the bookshelf, although it seemed pointless considering the mess.

"That makes sense. So what are we looking for?"

"Your guess is as good as mine. Something that might give us a clue to what has happened to Gunter. Documents, memory cards, appointment book, address book . . . anything. Start with his desk and work your way around the room. I'll begin in the bedroom."

Hank paused in the doorway. Gunter's bed had been slashed with a knife. Even the pillows had been ripped apart. Chicken feathers wafted everywhere and Hank couldn't help but remember last night's dinner. Darok 9 poultry was a valuable commodity—meat, eggs and feathers. He sneezed several times as he made his way across the room to the chest of drawers under the window. Gunter's green boxer shorts were hanging out of the half-open top drawer and socks and sweaters were thrown on the floor. Hank opened the remaining drawers one by one. They were empty.

He sighed and looked around. The furniture was sparse, as it was in most people's homes in Darok 9. A chair was angled in the corner and a small cupboard, doors open, stood next to the bed. Hank searched the items strewn across the floor and felt inside the cabinet. Nothing. He sat on the bed, sending more chicken feathers into the air, and stared at the purple patterned fabric of the hideous drapes. Perhaps something could be hidden in the lining? Hank got to his feet, and began to feel up and down the fabric. Nothing. He was disheartened. Whoever had trashed Gunter's apartment had probably found what they were looking for.

"Hank, come here, quickly!" Rachel shouted from the other room.

Hank raced into the living room. Rachel stood by the upturned coffee table holding a small wooden box that was elaborately carved and decorated with painted flowers. The lid had been wrenched off and now hung by one hinge. Rachel opened the box carefully, revealing a red velvet interior and a small ballerina sprung on a central pedestal.

"What is it?" Hank asked.

"It's one of those old music boxes from Earth. Mother's got one locked in the bank vault. It's been passed down through our family, remember? Whoever trashed the apartment tossed it on the floor and broke the lid." She pointed to a small hole in the side. "A key goes in there and you wind it up. Let's see if it still works."

"You think Gunter's key belongs to that?"

"Could be. Let's see."

Hank pulled out the tiny brass key that Will had found in Gunter's briefcase and placed it in the palm of Rachel's hand. "If this is what the key belongs to, I can't imagine it will have any significance. The box probably belonged to Gunter's great-great-grandmother."

Rachel pushed the key into the lock. It slipped into place easily. Slowly she turned the key clockwise until it wouldn't wind any further. The plastic ballerina rotated slowly and a delicate ballad played.

Hank groaned. "Well, I guess that's it, then. We've come to a dead end."

"Why would Gunter carry around a key to a music box in his briefcase? It seems odd, don't you think?"

"Sentiment...he loved his grandmother...who knows? We're wasting time here. Let's go home and take another look at the paperwork in his briefcase."

"No, wait, Hank," said Rachel, grabbing his wrist. "What's the name of that tune?"

Hank shrugged. "I've heard it before, but I couldn't tell you what it's called. I think you're trying to make a connection where there isn't one."

"But I *may* be right," said Rachel. "The name of the song might tell us something."

"And it might not," said Hank. "Gunter's a sentimental old man. Maybe the box is just some family possession he valued."

"Then why didn't he keep the music box and the key in a safe place...like Mother keeps hers in the bank?" Rachel looked at him with huge pleading eyes. "You must admit it's worth pursuing."

"I don't know, Rach..." Hank thought for a moment. He knew that in her current mood, his sister wouldn't take no for an answer. "Okay. We'll take it with us and see if we can find out the title of the song."

Rachel had already slipped the box into her bag and was on her way to the door. "We can meet up with Will at Maddie Goren's home. She'll easily be able to search for the song title on the computer."

Hank sighed. He stepped on several of Gunter's possessions as he tried to find a pathway to the door. He was pleased to see his sister so hopeful, but deep down he thought the music box was a waste of time.

Chapter 5

Will jogged up to Madeleine Goren's apartment complex in Apollo Square, excited that he had an excuse to visit her. Maddie was always so much fun to be around and she was pretty, too. Not only that, but she understood computers better than most kids their age.

Will opened the white picket gate and walked under the pink striped awning up to the front door. His heart jumped when he saw Maddie at her computer through the ground floor window. He tapped lightly on the glass. Maddie beamed and waved back, then disappeared from sight.

The front door opened. "Hi, Will, it's good to see you. Got any more mysteries to solve?" She laughed.

Will laughed with her. Her happy nature was infectious. "Actually, I do...and I was hoping you could help." He produced the memory cards from his pocket and held them out to her.

Maddie studied him and then the memory cards. Her face lit up. "Have you *really* got something that needs investigating?"

Will nodded.

"Come in," said Maddie, pulling him into the hallway. "Tell me more. It's only the first week off school and I'm already *so* bored." Her long auburn ponytail swung from side to side as she bounced into the living room.

Will followed her. "I know the feeling. There's not a lot to do in Darok 9," he agreed. "I was pleased when Uncle Hank asked me to research M.J. Rigby."

"Who?" asked Maddie.

"M.J. Rigby. We don't know who that is, or was, and we need to find out."

Maddie leaned forward to listen to him. "Why?"

"It's a long story, but we think he or she might be connected with Dr. Schumann's disappearance."

The surprise showed on Maddie's face. "The guy your mom works for has gone missing?"

Will nodded.

"Are you sure? It's not been on the Net News."

"I know. Uncle Hank's trying to keep it quiet while he does a bit of investigating. But if Schumann doesn't turn up by six o'clock tonight my uncle is going to see Commander Gillman."

Maddie sighed. "I suppose that after the David section turned bad last year, your uncle must find it hard to trust anyone on the Darok 9 security force."

Will smiled. "You've pretty much got Uncle Hank figured out," he said, shuddering with the memory of how he had nearly died when the David section was working with the enemy. "Mom's pretty worried about the doc. He seems to have vanished. Then, after we took his briefcase from the Pathology Department last night, someone broke into my house."

Maddie's eyes were wide with interest. "Gee, when I

asked you if you had something worth investigating, I wasn't thinking of something like this! What did they take?"

"Memory cards that contained records of body scans done in the Pathology Lab in the last month, and a file marked M.J. Rigby. That's the strange part, though, because the file was empty."

Maddie pointed at the memory cards in Will's hand. "So what are those?"

"Copies of the originals. Luckily I made them before I went to bed."

"Nothing lucky about it," said Maddie, grinning broadly. "Just quick thinking and good sense, Will Conroy."

Will blushed. He wasn't used to such open compliments, especially not from Maddie, but it was nice that she thought him smart. Trying to appear unaffected by her comments, he continued with the story. "We took a quick look at the records last night hoping to find out why the doc might have disappeared, and who M.J. Rigby was. But nothing in the records gave us any clues."

Maddie grabbed the cards from Will's hand and inserted one into her optical computer. Her eyes sparkled. "So let's see what *I* can find out!" She pulled out the chair and plunked herself into the seat.

Will smiled. He knew that she'd rise to the challenge. Maddie clipped a small microphone to her pale yellow sweater and began giving instructions to the optical computer.

"What are you doing, exactly?" he asked.

"Trying to establish any patterns between people who died last month and the body scans and blood tests performed by Dr. Schumann and your mother."

"Patterns?"

"You know—things that are the same."

"Oh, right." He watched her intently and listened as she instructed the computer to create charts and graphs, and keyed in information from the files. She sorted the names by personal statistics, diseases and other information. He could tell that she was thoroughly enjoying playing detective.

A few minutes later Maddie swiveled around in the chair and grinned at him. On the screen was a list of similarities between the cases.

"I'm impressed," said Will, leaning forward to read the results. "All these people died from diseases—either heart attacks, pneumonia or cancer. All were between 64 and 82, and sixty percent were male."

"There doesn't seem to be anything sinister or abnormal about any of that," commented Maddie. "*But* I guarantee M.J. Rigby isn't listed anywhere in the records. Are you sure you got the name right?"

Will nodded. "Positive. So now what?"

Maddie smiled mysteriously and set to work again. She ejected the memory cards and logged onto the Moon Net. "Well, let's see what comes up when I search Darok 9 birth and death records for that name."

Will watched, eagerly anticipating the results.

She sighed. "There's no record of an M.J. Rigby born in Darok 9."

A tap sounded on the window. Will looked over his shoulder to see his mom and Uncle Hank waving through the glass.

"I'll get the door and you keep going," he said to Maddie.

"That's fine," she mumbled and continued to work.

"So, Maddie...Will says you haven't found anything suspicious," said Hank, walking into the Gorens' living room.

Maddie shook her head. "Sorry, Mr. Havard. How about you?"

"Nothing," said Hank. "Although my friend Mac has suddenly ended up in hospital."

"I'm sorry to hear that, Mr. Havard," said Maddie. "I know he was a close friend."

"What happened to him?" asked Will.

"Don't really know all the details yet. Rumor has it that he overdosed."

"Mackenzie Stewart?" said Will. "The same guy that wouldn't even take an aspirin for a headache? Doesn't that seem a bit suspicious?"

"Indeed," agreed Hank. "I'd already come to that conclusion. I'll pay him a visit later."

"All the lab reports and body scans that we've checked are normal," said Maddie. "The only strange thing so far is that we can't find any record of an M.J. Rigby in Darok

9. No birth record and no death record. It's as if the person didn't exist."

"Perhaps Rigby is an alias," suggested Will, "or a code for something completely different."

"How about we try something else?" said Rachel, producing the music box from her bag. "See if you can find out what this tune is."

Will frowned. "Mom, this is serious stuff here. Let's not waste time listening to music."

"This *is* connected to Gunter's disappearance, Will," she snapped. She turned the key in the box and set it on the desk to play the gentle tune. "As you can see, the key you found in Gunter's case fits perfectly."

"Great going," said Will.

Maddie recorded several bars of the music onto the optical computer memory and then ordered a search. Within seconds the computer screen announced: *Blue Lullaby. Music by Kathryn Falkner.*

Rachel groaned. "Looks like you were right, Hank."

"Sorry, Rach, I thought you were trying to make a connection where there wasn't one."

"Lyrics," she said, as if thinking aloud. "Pull up the lyrics to the song, Maddie."

"Sorry, Mrs. Conroy. That's another dead end. The tune doesn't have any words."

Will sighed. "We're still no closer to finding out who he was or when he died, or why the doc has disappeared."

"But I just *feel* that we're on the right track," said Rachel determinedly. She slipped the music box back in her bag. "I'm sure Gunter left us a clue. The box must be important. Otherwise why would he have carried the key around in his briefcase?"

"Perhaps he's just a sentimental old man," said Maddie.

"That's what Hank suggested," said Rachel, "but I just don't believe that's all there is to it."

Will noticed Hank's glazed expression. "What are you thinking, Uncle Hank?"

"What about searching the birth and death records in the other Daroks?"

"I'm one step ahead of you," Maddie replied. "That's what I was doing when you walked in. It'll take me a minute."

"Why would someone steal an empty brown folder if not to prevent us from finding out about M.J. Rigby?" asked Hank.

Rachel's eyes grew wide. "Did you say *brown* folder?"

"Yes," said Hank. "Is that significant?"

She looked suddenly pale. "All of the other folders you picked up were cream, right?"

"Sure," Will cut in. "So what's a brown folder, Mom?"

Rachel paused and bit her lip. "I think I know where we'll find M.J. Rigby."

"You do?" said Hank and Maddie in unison.

"Well, don't keep us in suspense, Mom! Where?"

Rachel shuddered noticeably. She drew in a deep breath. "In one of the Darok 9 cryotanks!"

"Rigby's been frozen?" questioned Will.

Hank slammed his hand down on the table in excitement. "So the brown folders are the records of those who were cryopreserved?"

Rachel nodded. "But why would that folder have been in with the regular pathology files?"

"It wasn't. It was in a heap of papers and folders strewn across the floor of Gunter's office. Someone had obviously been through all the filing cabinets before I arrived. Whoever it was probably found what he was looking for, removed the contents and dropped the empty folder on the floor."

"Then why break into our house to get the folder if they left it behind in the lab in the first place?" asked Will.

"Because we were taking too great an interest in Schumann's disappearance and our intruder didn't want us to find out about M.J. Rigby." Hank leaned over Maddie. "Any luck locating Rigby in any of the other Daroks?"

"Here are the results coming up now, Mr. Havard."

"There it is! Micky J. Rigby," said Will excitedly.

Hank smiled. "I knew it! He lived in Darok 2 and died at age 39 in 2118—three years ago."

"No more information on him?" asked Will.

"That's your lot for now," replied Maddie. "There's no mention of cryopreservation. I'm sure I can find out more, but it will take time."

"The hospital computer records might tell us something quickly," suggested Will.

"Do you have access to the Cryolab computer files,

Mrs. Conroy?" Maddie grinned and added, "I've learned my lesson about hacking into secure Netsites after I got caught by the security force last year."

"Sure," Rachel replied. "It's part of my job to enter new cryopatients' information into the data base—but I don't ever remember seeing a Micky J. Rigby on the list."

"Don't forget that he died three years ago, Mom. That's before you started working in the Pathology Department."

"True," said Rachel. "And I usually access the data base only to add new files, not to browse the entire patient list."

"Well, what are we waiting for?" asked Hank. "I think this calls for a return visit to the hospital." He looked at his watch. "Sorry, I can't go. It's already two o'clock and we haven't even stopped for lunch." He sighed. "I have to be on the first Bullet to Darok 10 in the morning and I haven't started packing. I'd also like to visit Mac before I go."

"No problem," said Rachel. "I'll access the records and check back with you before six."

"Don't worry," said Hank. "I haven't forgotten your deadline. If we don't find out anything about Gunter by six, I'll visit Gillman myself."

"I can go to the hospital with you, Mom," said Will, knowing that she might nervous about returning to the Pathology Department.

Rachel shook her head. "Thanks, but I'll be fine. I have to go to work on Monday anyway, so I might as well get over my nerves right now. You'll do better here helping Maddie. Search the Net for anything you can find out on Micky J. Rigby. We need concrete information to take to Richard Gillman this evening. Let's see if we can get it."

* * * * *

Rachel played nervously with the ends of her hair as she stepped out of the elevator in the hospital basement. Suddenly she didn't feel so brave. She wished that she'd allowed Will to accompany her. Sucking in a deep breath, she walked past the Cryolab without even a glance at it, through the Pathology Department and into Gunter Schumann's office.

After a few moments of hesitation, Rachel sat down at his computer. This felt wrong, but she convinced herself she was doing it for Gunter. She adjusted the position of the keyboard, entered her password and waited to access the Cryolab files. The menu appeared on the screen.

Rachel scrolled through the options and selected 'Patients.' She stared in disbelief at the almost-blank screen. There was only a list of file numbers. Where were all the patient names and the detailed personal records Gunter kept for each patient? She'd entered a lot of that information into the data base herself. The information must have been deleted.

Her heart pounded. Someone had already accessed

the files. But who? Only she, and Gunter, and a handful of senior hospital officials had passwords to access the files. But of course that made no difference. Even Madeleine Goren had enough technical expertise to hack into the hospital computer system if she wanted to. Anyone determined enough to delete this information could easily do so.

She pulled up the computer log and checked for recent activity. "One hour ago!" she yelled. "Someone deleted the files from the network only one hour ago!"

Rachel looked up nervously. A chill ran down her spine, just as it had the night before. Was someone watching her? She grabbed her bag, strode quickly out of Gunter's office and through the swinging doors. The corridor was empty. Relieved, she almost ran to the elevators. But as she reached the Cryolab door, she stopped. *Was* Micky Rigby in one of the Darok 9 cryotanks? There was only one way to solve the mystery, but did she have the guts to go through with it? She shook her head. What was she thinking? She hated the place! She took two more steps and then stopped again. Her curiosity was getting the better of her.

Each cryotank was labeled with the names of the fifteen patients preserved inside, and now that the information had been deleted from the hospital records this might be the only way to find out if Micky J. Rigby *was* in one of those tanks. Even though she hated to admit it, she was curious to know what he looked like. She approached the Cryolab door. Did she have the courage to go inside?

Rachel's hand trembled as she punched in her code and pushed down on the door handle. She entered the room, turned on a couple of lights and looked around. The Cryolab was peaceful inside and undisturbed just as before.

Slowly she made her way over to the enormous tank closest to the door, and straining on her tiptoes she read the names inscribed on a plaque on the outside. There was no Micky J. Rigby.

Rachel moved on to the second tank and ran her index finger down the list as she read. Her heart beat faster. The fifteenth name was *Micky J. Rigby*. She was right. The man *was* here—frozen in tank 2!

Rachel walked around the tank, counting until she reached cylinder 15. She exhaled slowly and daringly looked up. The face of a good-looking woman stared back at her. Rachel gasped. She'd expected a middle-aged man! The woman had fine, elegant features: a perfectly even chin, straight nose and high cheekbones. Her open eyes seemed to smile.

"*You're* Micky J. Rigby?" she muttered. "But you're—a woman!" Rachel stood transfixed for a few minutes. They had all assumed that Micky was a man, but why shouldn't Micky be a woman?

She turned toward the enormous Cryolab safe. Inside, the personal belongings of patient 15 were stored in box 15. At least the safe was secure—only she, Gunter and Commander Richard Gillman at Darok 9 security force had an access code. The safe was opened only when a new patient was frozen and a few choice personal items were locked away for the patient's return to life. Perhaps Micky J. Rigby's box held photographs and family records that would provide clues.

Rachel punched in the four-digit access code. She struggled to open the heavy door, groped for the light switch, and stepped inside. Rachel stared at the wall of boxes in front of her. She strained to read the labels, her head pounding with tension. Tank 2, drawer 15 was at the end of the second row. The name plaque read M.J. Rigby. She swallowed hard. The box had been forced open and the lid was bent so that it no longer closed properly.

She pulled the box out, lifted the lid and felt inside. It was empty. "Gone," she muttered. "Her personal belongings are gone." Her heart beat faster. Someone had removed Micky Rigby's personal belongings—but who and why? Who was this M.J. Rigby? Why was she so important?

Rachel pushed the box back into position, her head spinning. She was leaving with more questions than she'd come in with. She turned, took two steps toward the door and screamed. Slumped in the corner of the safe was a pale and lifeless body. It was Gunter Schumann.

Chapter 6

Maddie thumped the table. "It's no good. I can't find any records from Darok 2 about Micky Rigby. I hate giving up, but it's an impossible task!" She sighed loudly as she pushed back her computer chair. "It's as if he never lived anywhere, never did anything, and never had any family. I'm taking a break. Are you hungry?"

"Always," said Will.

"Good. Mom made some cookies. Want one?"

"Sure." Will followed her into the kitchen and leaned against the countertop. "We'll just have to tackle the problem from a different angle." He grabbed a cookie from the plate. Hmm. Smelled deliciously like oranges.

"I hope your mom has had more success with the hospital data base," said Maddie.

"We'll have to wait 'til she gets back to find out," said Will, grabbing another cookie and shoving it into his mouth, whole. He chewed it quickly and added, "In the meantime, isn't there somewhere else we can get information?"

Maddie paused. "Okay, besides family members and the hospital, who else would keep records of people who have been cryopreserved? Do you think the Darok 9 historical society would?"

"That would depend on who has been frozen," said Will, taking a third cookie off the plate. "The historical society would probably keep records of people who have been important to our survival on the Moon."

Maddie nodded. "True. Everyone knows that only a select few scientists, doctors and military leaders are cryopreserved because there just isn't space in the cryotanks for everyone."

"That's it!" shouted Will, almost choking on his mouthful. "I'll bet First Quadrant Military Command keeps records of which scientific, medical and military minds have been preserved."

"You're right." Maddie's face brightened. "Particularly if a person were working on something classified when he or she died."

"I'll bet anything Micky Rigby was a scientist or a doctor in Darok 2. Perhaps he was working on something important when he died," said Will.

"There's no way I can hack into the First Quadrant military data base. The military installed new protection devices after I hacked into the system last year," said Maddie, blushing. "Even the best hacker wouldn't get in now."

"So how can we find out?"

Maddie stared at Will. Her eyes sparkled. "The good old fashioned way, of course!" She put her cookie down on the countertop without having taken a bite and brushed the crumbs off her hands. "Where are we likely to find military paperwork?"

"First Quadrant Military Command Headquarters," guessed Will.

Maddie nodded. "You got it. Are you coming?"

Will frowned. Surely she wasn't serious! "But that's in Darok 10! Besides, getting into their records department would be just as impossible as hacking into their data base!"

"You want an excuse to see your uncle's new lab, don't you?" Maddie persisted.

"But he's not going until tomorrow!"

"So? We'll get a head start on him. Besides, your Uncle Hank is already looking for Dr. Schumann. He'll help us get the cryopreservation records."

Will bit his lip. "It'll be difficult convincing Mom to let me go."

"Your dad's already there, isn't he?"

Will nodded.

"Well...call up your dad and get his permission." Maddie grinned and added, "He'll talk your mom into it. Mine always does."

"It *is* the quarterly vacation," said Will, trying to convince himself that it was a good idea. "Dad did want me to see Darok 10...and with Uncle Hank there as well this week, it's great timing."

"Good," said Maddie. "I need an adventure. Mom and Dad will let me go if they know we're visiting your father."

"I'll have to go home and make the arrangements. Mom should be back in an hour or two. Got a Bullet timetable?"

"Let's take one of the new improved hoppers," said Maddie. "Everyone says they're much smoother than the old hoppers. I've been dying to see how they work *and* it'll be much more fun than taking a Bullet. I'd rather look at the lunar surface, boring as it is, than travel through a dark tunnel for hours."

"But the new hopper still takes longer than the Bullet and it's more expensive," said Will. "Besides, we can't do anything until Monday morning, anyway."

Maddie smiled. "We can't? I bet that First Quadrant Command has a limited staff over the weekend. It's the perfect opportunity."

"You're making it sound so easy and it's not going to be," said Will, worried that Maddie hadn't thought the whole thing through.

Maddie grinned. "Twenty ration points from the travel card for the hopper and a load of fun, or fifteen points for the Bullet and a dull, uncomfortable ride? Which is it to be?"

Will studied her for a moment, then laughed. Maddie was determined to go. "Put like that...is there any choice? Okay, hopper it is. My parents won't mind five extra points. I rarely go anywhere on this boring Moon."

"Any idea when the next hopper leaves?"

"Dad sometimes catches the six o'clock on a Sunday night."

"That gives us two hours. Think you can be ready?"

"Sure. I'll call Mom if she's not back when I get home.

I'll see you at Port One at five-thirty."

"Good. I'll call ahead and reserve tickets." Maddie said as she walked Will to the door. "Don't be late," she shouted after him.

Will turned around at the end of the path and smiled. "I'll be there before you."

* * * * *

Rachel's head pounded. Every muscle in her body tensed as she approached Gunter Schumann's motionless figure slumped in the corner of the safe. She knelt beside him, tears welling in her eyes.

"Gunter? Are you okay, Gunter?"

There was no response. Her hand quivered as she felt for a pulse in his neck. It was weak—but it was there! He was alive!

Rachel sniffed back the tears and rummaged in her bag for her VisionCom. She had to call Hank. Then she remembered—she was in the hospital basement where she could never get a Com signal. She would have to go up to the foyer to call him. "I'll be back with help, Gunter. I'll get you out of here...I promise," she whispered, getting to her feet.

Something sharp and pointed poked into her ribs, making her drop her VisionCom and her bag. "Ouch! What the...?" She looked down and saw a laser dug into her side. She gulped and slowly lifted her hands above her head. In the low light she could barely make out the figure pointing the weapon at her.

"Mrs. Conroy, what a touching reunion with your boss. It's so nice to see you again."

Rachel's heart stopped. The chilling voice was one she knew well. It had been firmly entrenched in her mind. This was the person who had nearly killed her son a year ago. "L-L-Lydia...Gr-Grant," she stammered.

"So good of you to find your tongue and remember my name, Mrs. Conroy. Or should I call you Rachel? I really feel we should be on a first-name basis by now."

"How dare you!" Rachel shouted. Anger boiled in the pit of her stomach as the whole nightmare from a year ago came rushing back. "I thought we'd seen the last of you. I thought you were..."

"Dead?" finished Lydia. She tossed back her head and laughed. "Wishful thinking, Mrs. Conroy."

Rachel's insides twisted into a knot. How had she survived the faulty sample of SH33 they'd given her? She and everyone else had obviously underestimated this evil woman.

"Please credit me with more intelligence, Mrs. Conroy! That sample of Hank's wonder drug you gave me—I had it tested first. You didn't think I'd just inject myself with SH33, did you?"

Rachel could hardly contain her anger. Lydia Grant had killed to get her hands on the drug. How dare she return! How could she have got back into Darok 9 unnoticed? "Dr. Schumann...he needs medical treatment. Please, let me get him help."

"No." Lydia snapped. She shook her head slowly. "He knows too much. No one gets in my way. He's lucky I didn't kill him instantly." She bent over, picked up Rachel's VisionCom and tucked it in her jacket pocket. "We don't want you making any calls, do we now?"

Rachel thought she might be sick and clutched her stomach. Because of this woman, someone's life was being threatened once again. Will had nearly died when Lydia Grant had callously injected him with unstable SH33 and now Gunter Schumann was near to death. Her twisted mind would justify anything—no matter how evil.

"Step out of the safe." Lydia waved the laser toward the laboratory out back. "We're going to take a walk."

Rachel opened her mouth to reply and then thought better of it. If she argued, Lydia would shoot Gunter without a second thought. The woman was mad. At least he was alive and if she cooperated with Lydia, she might be able to help him.

"Don't forget that Gunter Schumann's survival depends upon your good behavior," said Lydia as if reading Rachel's thoughts. "Now walk to the door and turn on the lights in the research lab."

Rachel nodded. She stepped inside the lab and flicked the switch. As her eyes adjusted to the harsh lighting, she turned to face her enemy, and gasped. She barely recognized Lydia Grant. Her long, dark, curly hair had been dyed vibrant red and cut into a short bob with long, fashionably pointed bangs. Rachel had to admit that despite Lydia's evil mind, her face was quite pretty now that her hair didn't obscure her fine features. Was it any wonder that she had managed to get past security at the hopper port? She guessed that Lydia had fluttered her long lashes and flirted with the guard to get through the checkpoint.

Lydia's lips curled in a sneer. "I can see that you're admiring my new looks." She laughed and tossed back her head. Then her face became angry and defiant, and her dark eyes grew cold and sinister. "Fill the jug on the countertop with water. You can give some to Schumann."

Rachel was sweating profusely. Her hands shook so much that she could hardly hold the jug under the running water.

"You can thank me for my compassion," said Lydia. "Water's scarce enough on this barren excuse for a world without me wasting it on you two."

Rachel muttered, "Thank you," fearful that Lydia might change her mind if she didn't show her appreciation. Even though SH33, Hank's wonder drug was slowly cutting the water consumption of the population, it took a long time to produce any quantity. Most Darok 9 inhabitants, Gunter included, had still not received a shot of SH33 and therefore needed to drink water regularly.

Lydia ushered Rachel back into the safe.

"Now what?" Rachel asked, setting the jug on the floor next to Gunter.

"You may give him a drink," replied Lydia, starting to close the safe door.

"Stop! Please!" Rachel screamed, blocking the doorway the instant she realized what Lydia was doing. "You're not seriously going to leave us in here, are you?"

"There's a ventilation system," replied Lydia coldly. "You won't suffocate."

"But we'll die without food and Gunter needs medical treatment. It might be ages before someone finds us."

"Then you'd better pray that someone does." Lydia's thin lips spread slowly apart into a twisted smile. "You're not going to be a problem are you, Mrs. Conroy? I am sure you know that I wouldn't hesitate to kill both of you right now. You shouldn't have been so keen to meddle in things that didn't concern you. Your brother was warned several times. But that's Hank, isn't it? Always got to solve a problem. Always has to play the good guy. Still, this may all work out to my advantage." She laughed again. "Now, if you would be so kind, Mrs. Conroy, step back. I have an appointment to keep."

Rachel stood to one side and watched in horror as the thick metal door slammed shut and sealed them in an eerie tomb. "You'll never get away with it!" she yelled, even though she knew that Lydia could no longer hear her.

Rachel pounded on the door and screamed as loudly as she could until her palms were sore and her voice was hoarse. She sank to the floor, dejected, fighting back the tears. The silence inside the safe suddenly consumed her. All she could hear was her own heavy breathing and Gunter's short rasping breaths.

She felt claustrophobic in the confined space. She forced herself to breathe deeply, but the walls seemed to be closing in on her, pressing and pushing her back into the corner. She clamped her hands over her ears and yelled, "Enough!"

In the low light she looked down at Gunter, lying on the floor next to her. She had to keep positive...had to shake herself out of this state. All was not lost. They were both alive, and Will or Hank would surely come looking for her in a few hours. In the meantime she'd focus on helping Gunter.

"There's no way I'm going to sit back and let you win, Lydia Grant!" she hissed. It was fighting talk, but deep inside she knew that their situation was grim.

Chapter 7

Hank acknowledged the four members of the Michael section who stood on guard outside Mac's hospital room. Each section of the Darok 9 security force was made up of clones who all had the same name but different numbers, and were identical not only in looks but also in demeanor. Their tight-fitting black suits, with a circular emblem emblazoned on the jacket pocket, set them apart from the general population.

All four Michaels looked at him in the same way and Hank wondered if each Michael knew what all the others were thinking. One of the Michael clones blocked Hank's route to the door. Hank read M3 on his jacket lapels.

"Identification," Michael Three demanded.

Hank showed him his ID and security clearance—another advantage of working for the First Quadrant military.

Michael Three stood to one side and tipped his head politely. Hank knocked lightly on the door of Room 27 and entered without waiting for a reply. He walked over to the bed and looked down at the ashen face of his dear friend.

"Hi there, mate," whispered Mac in a scratchy voice. "Thanks for coming. I expect I look horrible."

Hank nodded. He dragged a chair from the corner of

the room and sat close to the bed. "I won't lie. You've looked better. How long are you going to be in here?"

"I'm improving fast. The doc says I should be able to go home tomorrow."

"Good news. So what happened? You hate pills, you spend your free time warning kids about the horrors of drugs and addiction, and you don't even take aspirin. I *know* you didn't overdose!"

Mac managed a smile. "You've known me a long time, Hank. Thanks for your faith in me. Of course I didn't overdose."

Hank patted his friend on the hand. "That's what I knew you'd say," he replied. "But if someone else drugged you this incident has a sinister twist. Has the security force questioned you?"

"Until I was exhausted," Mac groaned. "Like I told them, I can't explain how I got here. One minute I was getting ready for bed, the next I was being carried out on a stretcher. I do remember feeling slightly nauseous when I got home from work, but I figured it was something I ate. It just doesn't make sense."

Hank bit his lip. He took a deep breath and decided to break the bad news gently. "A lot of things don't make sense. Dr. Schumann disappears, then I'm threatened in the alley behind my sister's house last night and you're drugged just before you were going to run that DNA test on the blood and the hair from the hospital carpet. I don't know how all these pieces fit together, but I think they're all related to Dr. Schumann's disappearance."

"Here's something to fit into your puzzle," Mac whispered, struggling to sit up. "I *did* run the DNA test."

Hank raised his eyebrows. "When?"

Mac cleared his throat. "Late last night—right after I left you. Randolph was still there working and he helped me get it done." Mac's already pale face turned a shade whiter. He gulped. "Seems as if someone was trying to silence me."

Hank perched on the side of Mac's bed so that they could talk in hushed tones. "What did you find out?"

Mac cleared his throat again. "I ran a test for a DNA match between the hair and the blood."

"And?" said Hank, barely able to wait for the answer.

"They don't match. The hair and the blood are not from the same person."

"Really?" said Hank. "I wasn't expecting that."

"I guessed the hair didn't belong to Schumann before I ran the test, since he is gray and the hair is red. The question was whether the blood belonged to him. I was able to get Schumann's DNA from Darok 9 records. More and more I realize how useful it is that the security force takes a sample of DNA from every newborn."

"And?" asked Hank, impatiently.

"It's Schumann's blood," replied Mac conclusively.

Hank sighed. "Oh no. I was hoping that wasn't the case. Who's hair is it?"

"No records matched."

"So we're looking for someone born outside Darok 9. Well, at least we have the proof that something happened to Schumann. That's if the proof still exists. "

"How do you mean?" said Mac.

"I expect your test results have been wiped from the computer files, and I'll bet you anything that the blood and hair samples that you left in the security force forensic labs have been stolen. If so, we won't be able to run any more tests and we'll have no proof."

"Come on, Hank. Those samples would be really hard for anyone to steal. Security's tight at headquarters."

Hank snorted. "Who are you kidding? We both know that even an amateur could break into security force headquarters and into the security force network . . . my sister and 13-year-old Maddie Goren did it last year!"

Mac scowled. "I know, but network security was tightened after that incident."

"Not enough, I fear."

"Judging by your expression you think we've stumbled onto something big...real big...don't you, Hank?"

"Something's going on, but unfortunately I don't have time to continue looking for answers. I'm leaving for Darok 10 tomorrow. I start my research in the new labs on Monday. The Darok 9 security force will have to continue any investigation, which will please my sister no end."

"I bet this has freaked her out," said Mac.

"She's tough, but yeah, she's pretty shaken by all of this. If we could just find Schumann...I hope he's okay."

"Tell you what, Hank. I'll see Richard Gillman personally when I get out of here. I'll get the security force stirred into action in your absence. We'll find Schumann."

Hank smiled. "Thanks, Mac. You're looking better already—you never could resist the challenge of a mystery, could you?" He got up to leave. "So why don't you spend the rest of your time in the hospital working out how you could have been drugged?"

Mac lay back against the pillows and stared at the ceiling. "That's a tough one. No one visited me that evening and the security force said there were no unidentified fingerprints in my apartment and no sign of pills or drugs...except in my body!"

"You've got plenty to think about, then," said Hank with a smile. He shook his friend's hand. "I must go and pack. Get well quickly and keep in touch. I'll check the Moon Net regularly for messages."

Hank closed Mac's door, smiled at the Michael section standing on guard, and walked briskly to the elevator. He glanced at his watch. It was already 5:20. He'd stop by his sister's home to see if either she or Will had learned anything more about Micky Rigby, and then go home and pack. With everything that Mac had just told him, he prayed that Gunter Schumann was still alive.

* * * * *

Will stood by the front door with a dark blue canvas pack at his feet. He rotated his watchband around his wrist and looked at his watch for the twentieth time. If he didn't leave for the hopper port in the next two minutes he'd be late. "Mom, where are you?" he groaned. She wasn't answering her VisionCom and he had left several messages.

Will sighed. His father had approved his trip to Darok 10 and seemed excited that he was coming to visit. Where was his mother? Part of him wanted to wait for his mom to get home so he could say goodbye, but the pull of Darok 10 was strong. Besides, Maddie would be waiting for him . . .

That was it. "Time's up," he said out loud. "I'm going." He scribbled a note to his mother and propped it against a vase on a table just inside the door.

Will locked the townhouse, tore across Kennedy Plaza, cut through the alley onto Armstrong and headed toward Aldrin Court. It was Saturday afternoon, always busy in Darok 9. He wove in and out of groups of people who stood talking under the powerful streetlights, greeting those he knew as he ran by.

Maddie was waiting at the hopper port entrance. She waved as he approached. "Knew I'd beat you!" she laughed, picking her pack off the floor and slinging it over her shoulder.

Will smiled. "Sorry...minor delay." He stood panting for a few seconds. "Mom never came home and never answered the messages I left on her Com."

"Hope she's okay," said Maddie matter-of-factly as they walked up to the ticket desk.

"So do I." Will frowned. "You don't seriously think

something's happened to her, do you? I mean...with everything that's been going on..." He delved into his pack for his wallet and shoved his travel card into the scanner.

"Twenty points deducted. You have three hundred and seventy points remaining on the card," the automated voice said. "Take your ticket from the machine and proceed."

"Thanks," said Will, even though there was no one to thank. He stepped aside to allow Maddie to pay and waited uneasily for her answer.

Maddie shook her head and took her ticket from the machine. "Your mom probably just forgot about the time."

"Yeah...and there's always such a weak signal in the hospital basement so she probably won't pick up my VisionCom messages until she leaves," Will said, realizing that he sounded more confident than he felt.

Maddie steered him by the elbow across the lobby. Will barely noticed as he was still thinking about his mom. Something just didn't feel right. Perhaps he shouldn't go to Darok 10 until tomorrow. He handed the guard his ticket along with his ID card.

"Will Conroy, eh?"

Will sighed and stood tall. "That's me."

The guard glanced at the photo on the card and smiled at him. "Okay, you're clear to proceed. The hopper to Darok 10 leaves from gate 4."

"Thanks," said Will, putting his card and ticket in his back pocket. He turned and looked at Maddie as she handed over her ticket. "I'm sorry, Maddie. I can't go until I've called Uncle Hank. I'll ask him to check up on Mom for me."

"Better make it quick. They've just announced boarding."

Will rushed across the lobby to the VisionCom booths, ferreted in his pack once more for his wallet, and inserted his ration card into the slot. Slowly he recited his uncle's Com number into the microphone. He could see Maddie pacing anxiously by the boarding ramp. He felt better the moment he saw his Uncle Hank smile at him on the screen.

"Hi there, Will, what's up?"

"Maddie and I are going to Darok 10. We've come up with a way to get more information on Micky Rigby."

"Oh?" said Hank. "What exactly...?"

"Dad said it's fine if we stay with him," replied Will, cutting him off in mid-sentence. "I'm just worried because I can't reach Mom. She's not answered my Com messages and I've not heard from her this afternoon."

"Will!" He turned and saw Maddie wave her arms at him furiously. "You're out of time, Will. That was the final call."

"Sorry, Uncle Hank, I've got to go. They've announced final boarding. Maddie's upset that I'm not at the gate."

"Don't worry. I'm on my way over to your place right now and I'll check on your mom. I'll see you tomorrow evening at your dad's and you can fill me in on what you've found out."

Will sighed with relief. "Thanks, I appreciate it. I knew I could count on you. Bye."

He grabbed his wallet from the shelf in the booth, tore back across the lobby and up the hopper ramp to where Maddie was anxiously pacing.

"Well?"

"Uncle Hank's on his way round to see Mom right now. He said he'll meet us tomorrow evening at Dad's."

She smiled. "That's great. I'm sure you'll feel much better about going." Maddie picked up her heavy pack and slung it over her shoulder. "Now can we *please* board this thing before it goes without us?"

Will followed Maddie through the hopper doors, still trying to catch his breath. He pushed his pack into an overhead compartment and sat down next to her in one of the thirty luxury seats. Stretching out his legs, he couldn't deny that the latest hoppers were certainly more comfortable than the old design and were even better than the Bullet carriages. The hopper attendant was already on her way up the aisle with pre-dinner snacks. Maddie had her tray down in anticipation.

Will buckled himself in, tipped his chair back and closed his eyes. An uneasy feeling gripped him as he thought about the day's events. Uncle Hank hadn't actually said that he'd heard from his mom, just that he'd check on her. Somehow it felt wrong to be leaving Darok 9. He tried to shrug off the feeling. Was it just that his mom had been so upset last night? Or was she really in trouble?

The hopper doors closed and Will felt the jerky movement of the craft backing away from the gate. He looked out of the window as they hopped away from the port on the uneven lunar surface. Suddenly the hopper rose fifteen feet in the air and he heard its six long legs folding under its belly. The engine sound changed. Will gripped his armrests as they sped away. Darok 9 was already a speck in the distance. It was too late for him to change his mind. Within a few hours he would be entering Darok 10.

Chapter 8

Hank ran across the cobbled plaza to his sister's home. An uneasy feeling swept over him when he saw that the house was completely dark. Not even a tiny light glimmered through any window, in stark contrast to the other townhouses which brightly illuminated the street. He looked at his watch. 5:40 p.m. Rachel should have been home by now.

A small white envelope protruded out of the mail box on the wall by the door. Hank relaxed. Rachel had left him a note. He ripped open the envelope and unfolded the paper.

My dear Hank,

You'll never learn! You were warned to keep out of what didn't concern you, but you chose to interfere. Now your sister is paying the price for your meddling. If you wish to see her again you will do exactly as I ask. Take a Bullet to Darok 10. Walk to the Galaxy Hotel on Saturn Avenue and check into Room 36 before 10:00 tomorrow morning. A reservation has been made for you. Come alone and wait there for further instructions. If you alert the security force in either of the Daroks, your sister will die.

Hank's hands shook as he scrunched up the typed note into a tight ball. At first he felt anger, and then fear. What sick joke was someone playing? He uncrumpled the paper and read the note again, hardly believing what he had read. Rachel was in danger and it was his fault. He should have taken her advice and reported Gunter Schumann's disappearance immediately to Richard Gillman. Now it was too late. He read the letter a second time. It wasn't signed, and yet there was something eerily familiar about the wording.

"My dear Hank," he read out loud. His stomach tightened. Who always said that? An image of his former lab assistant flashed through his mind. "Lydia!" he gasped, recalling her dark eyes and evil laugh. "It has to be Lydia! Why didn't I realize? Everything that has happened carries her mark."

His mind raced through the events of the past twenty-four hours. He grimaced and growled through his teeth. Now he realized that it was Lydia who had threatened him in the alleyway. He knew he'd recognized something about the person . . . it hadn't been a man at all. It had been Lydia's short thin frame, and her piercing eyes peering at him through the mask. And the voice on Schumann's VisionCom...although disguised, it had seemed familiar at the time. Why hadn't he realized all this before? "Because you thought she was dead, you idiot!" he screamed at himself. "You trusting, naïve fool, Hank Havard!"

The insane woman had nearly killed Will last year and

was once again threatening his family. He paced back and forth. Rachel was in real danger.

He turned in circles looking at the sky through the dome of the Darok. "Why? Why would she do this?" he yelled. What could she want so badly that she would return to Darok 9, kidnap Gunter Schumann and threaten Rachel? Was she simply looking for revenge or was she working with the backing of the other three quadrants like before? Was the security of the First Quadrant Daroks at stake?

Hank crumpled up the paper and threw it on the street in anger and frustration, then thought better of it. He picked up the note and slipped it into his jacket pocket. He couldn't let anyone else find out about this...not yet...not until his sister was safe.

"Think, Hank," he said out loud. "Don't let Lydia get the better of you. Think—think hard. Two people's lives depend upon what you do next."

He had only two choices. Neither seemed sensible. If he contacted the security force of either Darok 9 or Darok 10, he'd place his sister in even more danger. Besides, Lydia had proved before that she was good at evading capture. But, if he went to Darok 10 without telling anyone, would he jeopardize his sister's life as well as his own?

Will! What about Will? Hank's heart sank. Will was on his way to Darok 10 with Maddie. The hopper had already left. Did Lydia know about Will's trip? Hank turned and raced across Kennedy Plaza. *I've got to get to him before she does!*

If he took the 7:00 Bullet to Darok 10, he'd arrive at 11 p.m. The new hoppers only took six hours. That would give him only half an hour to disembark and cross Darok 10 in time to meet Will's 11:30 hopper. The lives of three people depended on him. He had less than an hour to get to the station. This was a monorail he could not miss.

* * * * *

Rachel ripped off a long strip of fabric from the bottom edge of her slip. She folded it into a neat square and carefully applied pressure to Gunter's bleeding head. He had a nasty gash, but thankfully his injuries weren't more serious.

Gunter was beginning to come around. Rachel knew that she had to keep him awake and alert for her own sanity as well as his health. She had been locked inside the safe for less than an hour but already the claustrophobic conditions were making her sweat profusely. Perhaps between them they could figure out a way to escape. At least the safe was ventilated and the temperature cool. She remembered Gunter telling her that the expensive temperature control systems were necessary to preserve any documents or valuables in the boxes. If she got out alive, she would track down the designer of the safe and thank him personally.

Rachel shuddered. *If? If* she got out alive? What was

she thinking? "When!" she screamed. "When I get out alive!"

Gunter muttered. Rachel leaned over him. "Gunter, how are you? It's Rachel Conroy."

Gunter's face creased into a feeble smile. "Rachel...where am I?"

Rachel struggled to lift his heavy frame to a sitting position. He was weak and dazed. She gave him a drink from the jug and brushed drops of water off his graying beard. He licked his dry lips and looked around the room. She followed his gaze first to the ceiling and then to the metal boxes on the opposite side of the room. He was becoming more alert every second. Rachel watched his face crumple as he realized where they were.

"It's okay," she said softly. "We'll get out of here."

She saw the confusion in his eyes. "How did I...we...get *in* here?"

"You were hit over the head by Lydia Grant."

"Lydia Grant?" He choked on the name, his face paling.

He struggled to sit more comfortably. It was amazing the rousing effect that Lydia's name had on a man who had looked almost dead minutes before.

"What's *she* doing here? I thought...thought Darok 9 was rid of her."

"We don't know what she's doing here. You've got to think back, Gunter. What were you doing before you were knocked out? You had just checked the Cryolab for the night. Was she in here? What was she looking for?"

Gunter massaged his forehead with his fingertips. "I'm sorry, Rachel. I can't remember a thing."

"Box 15 has been forced open." Rachel pointed to the wall opposite. "I think it belongs to a woman by the name of Micky Rigby. Do you remember that name, or anything about her?"

His mouth tightened and he shook his head a second time. "Sorry," he repeated, his voice cracking. "My mind's a complete blank." He avoided her gaze.

Rachel didn't believe him for one minute. Gunter was not a convincing liar. What did he know? She sat down beside him and sighed heavily. "It'll come back to you, I'm sure."

"How did you come to be in here with me?" Gunter asked. He grimaced and shifted his position.

"It's a long story," said Rachel. "I'll save it for later. For now we have to concentrate on getting out of here."

"You're optimistic," said Gunter, massaging his temple again. "The walls are built of two layers of solid steel with a foot of concrete in between."

"I didn't for one minute think we could break out of here," Rachel replied. "I was thinking about hitting Lydia over the head with something when she comes back to check on us."

Gunter snorted at her. "I'm sorry to dampen your spirits, my dear, but I don't think Lydia Grant will be coming back any time soon."

"Why do you say that?" asked Rachel.

"The woman is heartless. We're lucky we're still alive."

Rachel's bottom lip quivered. Gunter was right, of course. Lydia Grant was insane. Unless she had some reason for keeping them both alive, she would not be returning. "Well, I'm not sitting back and wasting away in here. There must be some way we can get a message to someone in the hospital." In desperation she opened her handbag on her lap and rifled through the contents. There had to be something she could use. Of course! She could call someone on her Com! Her heart sank. "Oh no, Lydia took my Com."

"Useless anyway," mumbled Gunter. "There's no signal down here." He closed his eyes and tipped his head back against the wall.

Rachel continued to pull out the contents of her handbag. She laid out her ration cards, keys, comb, Hank's decoder . . . Hank's what? "I don't believe it!" Rachel screamed with delight. She picked it up and scrambled to her feet. "I've got a military decoder! Hank handed it to me when we went to your apartment and I never gave it back to him. We can get out of here!" Rachel waved it at Gunter and then pointed it at the door. Nothing happened. "Come on, work, will you!" she banged it angrily in the palm of her hand.

Gunter shook his head. "Give it up, Rachel," he said. "It won't work from the inside."

"But it has to," said Rachel, clicking the decoder again.

"Decoders have to connect into the electronic slot in the code panel, which is usually on the outside. The device doesn't work if you just point it."

Rachel looked at Gunter. His eyes were filled with sadness, his mouth curved downward. He didn't have to say another word. Rachel quietly placed the decoder back in her bag and zipped it up. She sat down again, her back against the door she couldn't open.

"It was a good thought," said Gunter. He patted her hand.

They sat in silence for a few minutes staring at the metal boxes built into the opposite wall.

"Of course," said Rachel, unzipping her bag again. "There's no reason why the decoder won't open the personal boxes inside this safe."

"But what good is that?" asked Gunter.

"There may be something in one of them we could use to get out of here." Rachel smiled at him weakly and took the decoder out of her bag. She was determined to keep their spirits up and their minds occupied. "It's worth a try. I've always wanted to know what valuables our cryopatients have stored in their boxes for their return to life."

Gunter chuckled. "When my grandmother was alive she was always telling me to use and enjoy all my possessions while I could. *'What good are they to you when you are dead?'* she would say. *'You can't take your things with you'.*"

"I guess she hadn't heard about cryonics when she said that," laughed Rachel.

"Well, she died ten years ago, just as significant breakthroughs were being made in cryonics research.

Even I wouldn't have imagined that we'd be so close to seeing it become a reality. So, what are you waiting for? Open up a box—any box!"

Rachel walked to the back wall and inserted the decoder into the key slot of the first box on the top row. The box glided forward from its space in the wall. Rachel lifted the lid, and standing on tiptoes, peered inside. She pulled out an envelope and sat back on the floor next to Gunter.

"Tank 1, Patient 1: Ruth McKenna." Rachel lifted the flap of the envelope and dug inside. "Let's see what we have in here. Memory cards containing records of birth, marriage, immunizations and medical procedures, family photographs and research memory cards."

"As expected," said Gunter with a grunt. "Nothing exciting or useful. If I remember correctly she was a brilliant young doctor."

"What did she die from?"

"Cancer—a type that we can now eliminate."

"Let's try another," said Rachel moving along the row to the second box. "Tank 1. Patient 2: Jimmy London."

"What's inside?" asked Gunter.

"Pretty much the same. An envelope containing family photos, a wedding ring and paperwork." She opened one of the documents. "The death certificate says he died from Hodgkins Lymphoma."

"Shame. That's also curable now," said Gunter with a grunt.

"I'm beginning to think that Will is right," said Rachel.

"How do you mean?"

"Will thinks that cryonics is the future of science on the Moon. But I'd hate to die and come back fifty years later when my family and friends were gone and everything had changed."

"But now...you think differently?" asked Gunter.

"Cryonics may not be for me, but if the lives of brilliant people are cut short by illness, and they want to be cryopreserved to come back to do more good for mankind... why not?"

"Well, well," said Gunter. He forced a smile. "I never thought I'd see the day when Rachel Conroy thought cryonics was a good thing. Pity that so many are still opposed to the idea. Perhaps it will become acceptable when technology proves that it's possible to bring someone back to lead a healthy life."

Rachel smiled. "And I don't doubt for one minute that my son will be on the research team that succeeds!"

"He's certainly determined and smart enough," said Gunter, banging the back of his head accidentally against the wall and wincing with the pain. "Ouch! Didn't realize that I'd been hit so hard."

"It was pretty bad," said Rachel, putting the envelope back in the box. She sighed. "I don't see any point in opening the rest of the boxes. I don't know what I expected to find. I'm sure they'll all contain family records, photographs and a few personal items." As she put the decoder back in her bag she noticed the music box. Dare she ask Gunter about it now that he had recovered somewhat? "Are you sure you don't remember anything that happened to you?" she asked gingerly. "What about the music box in your apartment?"

"Music box?" Gunter flinched noticeably.

"The one that has a ballerina in it."

"Oh, that one," said Gunter. "That was my great-*great*-grandmother's. How do you know about the music box?"

"Hank and I found it in your apartment. We went there hoping to find clues that would help us find you. In fact . . ." she said, delving into her bag, "I have the music box right here!"

Gunter's eyes widened and his hands shook as he took the box from her hands. "Does anyone else know you have this?"

"Just Hank," she replied, deciding not to mention Will and Maddie.

Gunter relaxed noticeably. "Good. That's good. Hank's trustworthy." He gripped the music box tightly in his lap.

"I have the key as well," said Rachel, producing it from her bag and dangling it by the red ribbon in front of him.

Gunter sprang forward with a groan and snatched the key from her grasp. There was a look of real fear in his eyes. His brow was furrowed and droplets of sweat dotted his forehead.

"Forget you ever saw this," he snapped, shoving the key into his pocket. "You don't know I have it and you don't know what it belongs to. Do you understand?"

Rachel stared at him without saying a word,

dumbstruck. Just a moment ago he'd been so relaxed.

Gunter's face reddened and he lunged forward, grabbing her face in his hands.

"You never saw it . . . do you hear me?" he said forcefully.

"Yes...yes...I...I hear you, Gunter," Rachel stammered, frightened by his intensity.

Gunter released her and threw himself back against the wall, panting heavily. "Good...that's good," he muttered in between gasps. "It's better that way. You'll see."

Chapter 9

"You've seen one crater, you've seen 'em all," said Will, stretching his arms above his head and yawning.

"Quit complaining," said Maddie, closing her notebook computer. "I'm sure people who lived on Earth said the same about trees, and yet *you'd* give anything to see one. Every crater is different. You just don't appreciate the beauty of the Moon, do you, Will Conroy?"

Will grinned at her. He wished he could think of a quick witty reply. She was right—the Moon did have a unique mystical beauty and he just wanted what he couldn't have.

A whining noise echoed in the cabin. The hopper's hydraulics were unfolding its six massive legs. They touched down with a thud. The rest of the ride was not as smooth as the vehicle clumsily jumped into the Darok 10 port. Will wondered how he had ever survived the lurching movement of the older generation of hoppers as they slowly jumped across the lunar surface, taking several days to reach a destination.

The hopper shuddered as it settled into position in the docking bay. The massive outer door of Bay 4 hissed as it sealed and pressurized.

Will glanced at his watch. "Not bad going. We're here twenty minutes early. Dad said that we should go to his apartment if he wasn't here to meet us. We should be able to find it easily."

"You're forgetting...this is Darok 10," Maddie reminded him as she unclipped her belt. "Haven't you paid attention to your dad's descriptions?"

"Sure, but I can't believe it's *that* much bigger than Darok 9."

"You may be in for a surprise. From what I hear, it takes well over an hour to walk from one end to the other. Darok 9 Net News says they've even got public transportation here!"

Will laughed. "Yeah, Dad mentioned it, but I'll believe it when I see it. It's probably just a few vehicles. The Net News is always trying to stir up trouble so that our Darok council agrees to street improvements. There are too many lazy people in Darok 9 who hate walking for ten minutes."

"Well, we'll soon see," said Maddie. "Let's go. They've opened the doors."

Will pulled down his pack from the overhead locker and stood back to let Maddie reach hers. He followed her to the front of the hopper and out onto the moving walkway. She set a brisk pace, overtaking other passengers as she headed to the hopper foyer. Will struggled to keep up, allowing the moving walkway to take him part of the journey. The sound of laughter and talking grew louder as he neared the end.

When he finally stepped off the walkway into the hopper foyer he could hardly believe his eyes. He stood next to Maddie, dazed by the huge number of people who dashed across the open area.

"I've never seen so many people, *and* it's late at night," gasped Maddie. "I should have taken Dad more seriously. This place is totally amazing!"

"Well, what are we waiting for? I don't see your dad, so let's find the exit to the street and take a look around." She heaved her pack onto her back and rushed off.

Will hesitated, pulling a piece of paper from his pocket on which he had written directions. "Maddie, wait!" He looked up at the sign flashing above him, which listed three different exits, and then again at his sheet. "Dad said we should take public transport from Comet Road or Saturn Avenue to get to First Quadrant Command Officers' Apartments," he muttered to himself as he read the instructions. "Maddie!" he called a second time, but she was long gone.

He ran after her, weaving through the massive crowd. This was like putting half the population of Darok 9 into one place. He burst onto Saturn Plaza. Maddie was nowhere in sight. Had she gone to another exit?

Will dropped his bag in utter amazement as he looked up at the huge dome of Darok 10. It had to be double the height of Darok 9, and its massive supporting struts seemed like long arms reaching into space. "Wow! Wow!" was all he could say. For the first time in his life he hardly felt like he was under a dome. The neon restaurant signs and powerful spotlights illuminated the tall buildings. The Moon was halfway through its fourteen days of darkness and yet this brightness seemed like daylight.

Will looked down at the surface of the street. On Darok 9 the streets were uneven, covered in lunar rocks, but the roads here were smooth. Small motorized vehicles hummed along. Each one that sped by had a different pitch, as if they were each singing a song. The vehicles were open-roofed and open-sided with wide running boards along the sides and rear. People jumped on and off, laughing and chatting, rushing in and out of buildings. He wanted to scream, "Slow down, everyone!" Where was the quiet life that he knew? Darok 10 seemed like a different Moon, not just a different Darok.

Will sat down on his backpack, soaking up the environment. No wonder his dad had wanted him to see this place. It was incredible. He and Maddie would have such fun exploring Darok 10. Maddie! He'd been so captivated by everything around him that he'd forgotten to look for her.

A bearded man stopped his vehicle in front of him. "Can I help you find your way somewhere?" he asked. He wore a bright orange cap with a long peak, "Nick" embroidered across the front. The letters DTTS were stamped on the chest pocket of his matching orange boiler suit and on the side of the white vehicle.

"What's DTTS?" asked Will, getting to his feet. He walked over to examine this new mode of transport.

"Darok Ten Transportation Service," the bearded man

answered in a raspy voice. "Nick at your service. You from another Darok?"

"Darok 9," said Will.

"Where are you headed?"

"First Quadrant Command Officers' Apartments. My dad lives here."

"The ComAp? I'll drive you. Hop in the Zoomer."

"Zoomer?"

"Yeah, this is a Zoomer. It started as a slang word." The driver jumped down awkwardly. He was plump and had difficulty lifting Will's pack into the open cargo container behind the back seat. "No one could think of anything original to call these motorized carts when they first appeared on the streets, but everyone was so amazed by how fast they could zoom along that the name kinda stuck."

Will laughed. He stepped onto the running board and hesitated. "I really need to find my friend, Maddie, before I go anywhere. We got separated in the hopper foyer."

"Young girl about your age with a ponytail and a backpack?"

Will nodded. "Sounds like her."

"She was walking down Saturn Avenue a minute ago. Looked like she was enjoying the surroundings. We can pick her up on the way."

Will smiled. That would be Maddie. He was willing to bet that the bright lights and the busy streets had also captivated her. She'd probably forgotten to check if he was even following.

Nick climbed behind the wheel. "Okay. I can have you at the ComAp in five minutes."

"How many points will it cost?" asked Will, taking out his travel ration card.

"Points? This is Darok 10. It'll cost you nothing," Nick coughed and cleared his throat. "Residents have transportation points deducted monthly. Visitors get free travel. It encourages trade and tourism."

Will sat down in the back. "Trade and tourism? That's something new."

As the car sped down Saturn, Will couldn't take his eyes off the lights and the buildings and the people...so many people even though it was nearly midnight. "A movie theater!" he shouted with glee. "I've always wanted to go to one. I've read about how kids on Earth a hundred years ago got to go all the time. And there are so many restaurants and stores here. I hope Dad'll take me to some of them."

Nick turned onto Jupiter Circle, honking impatiently at pedestrians crossing in front of him. Will gripped the metal handrail as the car cornered sharply.

"Zoomer's a perfect name. These things are fast," said Will. "Can anyone buy a Zoomer?"

Nick shook his head. "No privately owned vehicles allowed in Darok 10."

"I guess there's no room for parking," said Will.

Nick nodded and drove the car into a cul-de-sac, pulling up outside a tall building that was dark but for a few lights.

Will frowned. "Are you sure this is the right place? It seems really dark for officers' accommodation late on a Saturday night."

"'Course I'm sure. I've lived here for years. You forget that it's everyone's night to party until the early hours. That's why the streets are so busy. A lot of the officers will be out at the club and won't be back for a few hours yet."

"Oh," said Will. He couldn't believe what a different life this was. In Darok 9 the streets would be quiet by now even on a Saturday. The Lunar Café was the only place to go.

Nick pulled Will's bag from the back and waddled down the path with it. Will followed. It was not until they approached the door that he remembered Maddie. He'd been so caught up with the lights and music and the crowds that once again he'd forgotten about her.

"We'll have to go back," he said. "I'm sorry, but we forgot to look for my friend."

"She'll find her own way here," Nick said confidently. He opened the door and motioned for Will to enter.

"No, I really must go back for her. I can't leave her walking about on her own."

"Sounds to me like *she* left you. Why don't you see if your father's here first, and then you can both go out and find her?"

"I suppose that makes more sense...since I'm already here," said Will, stepping through the doorway into a wide hallway. "His apartment is 5D."

The door slammed behind him and a distinctive heavy clunk signaled an automatic lock clicking into place. Will turned. Nick drew a short black laser from his pocket.

What was happening? Will's heart quickened. He backed away from the door into the empty hallway, staring at the DTTS driver who had befriended him. Was he being robbed? Will pulled out his wallet. "Here, take my ration cards...take my watch...they're yours," he stammered.

"Ration cards? What would I want with them?" said Nick, lifting off his hat and brown wig.

Will stared in horror at the elegantly cut bright red hair that was suddenly revealed. What was happening here?

There was a loud rip as Nick yanked off his beard, laughing loudly.

Will gasped. This was no man! Fine feminine features that seemed frighteningly familiar faced him. Was it possible? And then came the laugh—a chilling sinister laugh that he knew and would never forget...a laugh that belonged to Lydia Grant. *Lydia Grant ...it couldn't be... could it?* Will felt as if he had been stabbed over and over again.

"Young Mr. Conroy," Lydia said, pointing the laser at him. "It's a *real* pleasure to see you again."

Will took a few seconds to find his voice. "Well, the feeling isn't mutual!"

"It must be quite a blow to your ego to see me here, I'm sure." Lydia unzipped the orange jumpsuit with her free hand and pulled out chunks of padding. "I had to rush to get here tonight before you. You should feel honored that you are so high on my list of priorities. You look rather pale."

"And you look hideous in that outfit!" Will retorted. "But I guess it matches the hairdo. You look like a carrot!"

Lydia tossed back her head and laughed wildly. She combed her long fingernails through her pointed red bangs. "My, oh my! Such a childish comment. You're a smart boy, Will. Couldn't you think of anything more original than that?"

Will blushed. It had been a feeble attempt on his part to say something insulting, but he was still reeling from shock. He had the sudden urge to run, but he'd heard the door to the street lock electronically. He eyed the four doors off the hallway. They were all closed. How could he run when he didn't know if they were also locked? Besides, Lydia had a laser pointed at him. He knew what this woman was capable of. Now was not the time to play hero.

"Seriously, Mr. Conroy...you and your family didn't think you'd be rid of me that easily, did you?"

Will backed away from her, his mind racing.

"What, no smart comment this time?"

The door by the stairs opened slowly. A tall tanned man walked into the hallway, a large weapon hanging from a brown strap over his left shoulder. Will could not draw his eyes from a wide raised scar, which ran straight across the man's forehead from one side of his head to the other.

Lydia looked at her watch. "It's time," she announced. "This is the renowned molecular scientist from Darok 2, Mr. Randolph Lazzar. You will accompany him without trouble. If you fail to cooperate, your mother will die a long and painful death back in Darok 9. Do I make myself clear?"

"My mother?" shouted Will. "You've got my mother? What have you done with her?"

Lydia's familiar twisted smile spread across her lips. She walked up to Will and ruffled his hair. "That's only for *me* to know," she whispered. "Now be a good boy and run along with Randolph. He'll take good care of you."

Will could take her taunting no longer. He spat in her face and kicked her in the kneecap with all his might. "You disgust me!"

Lydia yelled in pain and staggered sideways. Lazzar rushed forward and threw Will to one side. Will hardly felt the pain as his head hit the wall. He smirked, taking great pleasure in knowing that he had inflicted some injury on the woman. He wasn't about to hide his satisfaction.

Lydia bent and rubbed her knee vigorously, her complexion turning deep red. Her eyes narrowed as she stood slowly upright to face him. She wiped the spit from her face, and quickly composed herself. "Like every good son...so protective of his mother. Pity you can do nothing to save her!"

Will's anger rose again. "You hurt my mother and I'll see that you pay for it. Do *I* make myself clear?" he screamed.

"Just like last time?" she snarled. "I think not. But *you'll* pay for that last stunt!" She motioned to Randolph, who clamped Will's wrists together with a metal band. "Get him out of my sight!"

* * * * *

Maddie stood at the Comet Road entrance to the hopper port. She turned in circles, looking up and down the street, and scoured the faces of the people going in and out of the lobby. How could she have allowed her excitement to get the better of her? Now she was paying for her mistake. Will was nowhere in sight.

Darok 10 was a different world. The sheer number of people was bewildering—never mind the flashing signs and hundreds of vehicles that sped past. Much as she hated to admit it, Maddie the adventurous and fearless fourteen-year-old was nervous. She had lost Will, didn't know Mr. Conroy's VisionCom number or street address, and felt totally out of her depth in this new world.

New world? Who am I kidding? This is Darok 10, not some other planet. They speak English here. Get yourself together, girl! Ask for help—you've got a tongue, haven't you? Go to the information desk. She turned to go back into the lobby.

"Maddie! Wait!"

She knew that voice. She swiveled around. "Mr. Havard!" she screamed with delight.

Hank raced down Comet Road toward her, suitcase in one hand and briefcase in the other, gasping for breath. "I'm so glad I caught up with you two. This whole thing is far bigger than we ever imagined! I'm just thankful you're both okay and I got here in time."

Maddie looked at him, not knowing quite what to say.

"Where's Will?" Hank asked.

Maddie felt suddenly hot. She knew that her cheeks must have turned a bright shade of red. "I'm not really sure, Mr. Havard."

"Not sure? What do you mean?" Hank asked.

"We kind of got separated."

"Kind of?" Hank repeated, raising his voice. "What do you mean by *kind of*?"

"I'm sorry, Mr. Havard. I got carried away by the lights and all the people and the whole feeling of this place, and I rushed ahead of Will...and then when I turned around I couldn't see him anymore."

Hank scowled. "When was this, Maddie?" He put his bags down, placed his hands on her shoulders, and looked into her eyes. "Think, Maddie. How long since you saw him, exactly?"

"It's been a while." She looked at her watch. "At least twenty-five minutes."

"Drat," said Hank. "I'd hoped to get here before you disembarked."

Hank's expression frightened her. His brow was creased with deep lines and he was breathing heavily. He paced back and forth in front of her.

"We landed twenty minutes early," she said in an effort to explain. "Is everything okay, Mr. Havard?" She wasn't sure she really wanted to hear the answer.

Hank shook his head. He took her by the elbow, picked up both cases with his other hand and steered her across the foyer. "Stay close to me," he whispered. "Before we go any further, let's check that Will isn't at another entrance."

There was no sign of Will at either the Saturn or Nebula exits. Maddie felt desperate. She knew she was to blame, and Hank's behavior was scaring her. She had never seen him so red-faced and anxious.

"Let's see," he muttered, gazing up at the street map on the wall. "Saturn is what we must avoid, and Comet will take us to Will's dad at the ComAp . . . so that's no good either. It'll have to be Nebula."

Maddie was confused by his reasoning. "Why *aren't* we going to meet with Captain Conroy at the ComAp?" she asked.

"I want to check we're not being followed first," he replied. "No more questions right now, please. Just keep quiet and stay with me."

Maddie stared at Will's uncle. Hank Havard was usually such a fearless man who didn't seem much older than herself. Tonight he'd aged ten years and seemed to be anxious and nervous. She followed quietly on his heels, more fearful every time he stopped and looked about. Had he found out what had happened to Gunter Schumann? Is that why he was worried about Will?

Hank caught Maddie's arm and shoved his way into the middle of a jovial crowd exiting the hopper port onto Nebula Square. He turned to her and said, "We're going to walk up Nebula with these people and cross the street at the corner. I want you to keep your head down and laugh and chat with me as though we're part of this party. When we get to the other side of the street, we're going straight into the movie theater."

Maddie nodded and stuck close by Hank's side. How difficult it was to be party-spirited when she was shaking inside. She was so busy pretending to be happy that she barely remembered crossing the street. She watched Hank swipe his entertainment ration card through the machine in the theater foyer. He grabbed their tickets for the midnight showing of *The Black Planet*, and led her to seats in the back corner of the darkened theater.

"We'll rest here while I think about what we should do next," he said, ushering her along the row.

So much for her first trip to a movie theater. Maddie hardly watched what was on the screen. They sat in silence. She felt awkward. Hank obviously knew a lot more than he was letting on. And what about Will? Was he in danger of some kind? She couldn't bear not knowing. He owed her an explanation.

"Mr. Havard," she whispered. "I need to know what's going on. You can't keep me in the dark any longer—it's not fair to me. I'm a wreck! *Please*, do you know something about Dr. Schumann? Is that why you're worried about Will?"

Hank sighed heavily. "I apologize, Maddie. My mind's in a whirl, and I'm trying to sort out the facts from my hunches. No, I haven't found Dr. Schumann." He gulped and paused. "I don't know where my sister is either, and now Will's gone missing too."

"But Will might have found his way to his dad's apartment by now."

"I hope you're right...and we'll check on that first, of course, but my gut is telling me otherwise." His hands shook as he unfolded the crumpled note and gave it to her. "I was left a message threatening Rachel's life if I didn't come immediately to Darok 10."

Maddie strained to read the writing in the dim light. "But you ignored the threats and called the Darok 9 security force anyway, right?"

"It's not as simple as that. The tone of this letter and everything that has happened in the last two days has Lydia Grant's mark stamped all over it. I should have realized it sooner."

Maddie gasped. "Lydia Grant? But she's dead . . . isn't she?"

Hank shook his head. "We all wanted to believe that she injected herself with my drug and died, but I'm almost certain that somehow she survived." He put the note back in his pocket. "You know as well as I do that if I don't check into the Galaxy Hotel on Saturn Avenue by ten tomorrow morning, she'll kill Rachel without a thought."

Maddie swallowed hard. "You think she's already murdered Dr. Schumann, don't you?"

"It's a possibility. And if she has Will as well..." He stopped, as if his thoughts were too horrible to say out loud. "Somehow this is all tied in with the Darok 9 Cryolab...and that's what I don't understand. Lydia may want my head after I made her look bad in front of the United Quadrants last year, but she's out for much more than personal revenge. If she's been in Darok 9 for the last two days, she could have killed us many times. But she chose to warn us and walk away...until now. My guess is that she has a much bigger plan and we somehow got in her way. She'll want to restore her reputation with the United Quadrants and secure her position in the enemy government. To do that, she's got to pull off something dramatic like last year's attack on the Darok 9 water system."

Maddie's chest tightened. "You're not thinking that she's out to destroy one of the Daroks, are you, Mr. Havard?"

Hank nodded. "I can't deny that it's crossed my mind more than once. In Lydia's twisted mind, the destruction of a Darok and the death of thousands would prove her loyalty to our enemy. And knowing her," he paused and took a deep breath, "she'll want me alive to witness it. But how would she do that, Maddie? How would she destroy a Darok? And how does the Cryolab tie in?"

"I have no clue. Have you thought about *which* Darok, Mr. Havard?"

"How do you mean?"

Maddie was one step ahead. "Well, Lydia Grant was

obviously in Darok 9, but she sent you rushing over here. Now you *think* that she is also holding Will hostage, so does that mean she's here in Darok 10? Maybe she used the threat of Will's safety to force his mother to come with her."

Hank didn't reply immediately. "You're a bright young lady, Maddie." He pursed his lips, obviously in deep thought. "Or...is that just what she *wants* us to think?"

"You've got me," said Maddie. "I don't follow."

"We're now dealing with several possibilities," Hank groaned. "Is Lydia Grant holding Rachel *and* Will? Are they here in Darok 10? Or is that what she wants us to believe so that we're busy looking for them while she does something diabolical back in Darok 9?"

Maddie bit her lip. "I'll bet anything that Micky Rigby would give us the answer."

Chapter 10

Will rubbed his wrists and glared at his captor.

Randolph Lazzar tossed the metal clamp high in the air, watched it fall, and caught it again. He gave Will a crooked smile. "I've been kind and released you this time, but you won't get another chance—so don't blow it. I'm not one to take pity on bratty kids. Any more trouble and both your ankles and your wrists will be clamped." He pointed to a mattress on the floor. "I should get some sleep, if I were you," he muttered, walking to the door. "You're gonna be here a while. There's a bathroom in the far corner."

Will sighed with relief when Lazzar closed the door and he was on his own. Sleep? The man had to be joking. How could he sleep after everything that had happened?

He walked slowly around his new surroundings, looking for any means of escape. The only window in the room was screwed closed and boarded up with wide planks of imitation wood. The gaps between the planks allowed in light, but were not wide enough apart for him to see out or for anyone to see him. Lazzar had marched him up several flights of stairs, so it would be a long way down to street level even if he did find a way out.

Two mattresses lay on the floor. The bedding smelled fresh and the pillows appeared to be new. Lydia had obviously prepared for his capture and had not stumbled on him by chance at the hopper port. But how did she know that he was coming to Darok 10? It had been a last-minute decision on his part. *Two mattresses,* he thought. Had she intended to kidnap Maddie as well? His stomach tightened at the thought.

He turned around and noticed an old computer sitting on a desk in the corner. He raced across the room, eagerly turned it on and scoured the menu. There was an extensive choice of games, but his hopes were dashed when he realized there was no connection to the Moon Net. He slumped in the chair, staring at the screen. "Idiot," he said out loud. Lydia was hardly going to allow him to send a Net message to Uncle Hank.

He stared at the icons on the blue screen and yawned. He was exhausted, but too worried to sleep . . . and right now he certainly didn't feel like playing games. He felt stupid about how he had ended up here. How could he have been so naïve and trusting of a stranger?

He looked at his watch. It was 1 a.m. Where was Maddie and what was she doing? He prayed that Maddie wouldn't fall into the same trap and get carried away by the lights and sounds of Darok 10. He could only hope she'd found his father at the ComAp and told him that they had got separated. With any luck his father would have the Darok 10 security force looking for him by morning.

That last thought helped Will relax. Exhausted, he lay on the bed hoping that he might fall asleep. With a fresh mind he would think more clearly and perhaps find a way out, or a way to let someone know where he was. But just as he closed his eyes a wave of doubts gripped him, and his eyes shot open again. How had Lydia known that he and Maddie had taken that particular hopper from Darok 9? Had Lydia done something to his mom? Is that why his mother hadn't returned his Com messages before he left Darok 9? He felt sick with worry. He didn't know how he could help himself or his mother, and he didn't know how he'd ever be able to sleep.

* * * * *

"Micky Rigby!" said Hank, rising from his seat in the Darok 10 movie theater. "Thanks, Maddie, you've put me back on course."

"I have? You're welcome, Mr. Havard. Glad to have helped." She threw him a confused expression.

Hank smiled for the first time in hours. "Lydia first threatened us when we started investigating Micky Rigby, so that's who we should focus on right now. Find out about her and we might find out what Lydia's up to. Let's go."

"Go where?" whispered Maddie.

"The ComAp," said Hank, moving toward the rear exit of the movie theater. "We need to see Will's father. Hopefully, we'll have shaken off anyone following us, but we'll take the back alley to be sure."

"Just when I thought I was going to see a movie for the first time in my life," muttered Maddie.

"You wouldn't have enjoyed it right now," replied Hank confidently. "I'll make it up to you—I promise."

At the rear exit, Hank peered into the alley and ushered Maddie through the door. "This will take us through to Comet Road. We'll have to walk some distance. The ComAp is down by the Bullet station—that's nearly a mile."

"We could take public transport," suggested Maddie.

Hank shook his head. "Sorry. I know you'd enjoy trying it, but we need to keep a low profile. It's Saturday night. The streets will be fairly busy for another hour yet. We'll be better off just keeping with the crowds than being visible in a zoomer."

"Zoomer?" questioned Maddie.

Hank gestured for Maddie to follow, deciding he'd explain later. He set off at a brisk pace down Comet Road, checking every few seconds that Maddie was keeping up with him. She was panting heavily, but doing her best. In the distance he could see the grand entrance to the Bullet station, dwarfing the surrounding buildings. Darok 9's station seemed miniscule in comparison. Hank guessed that within the next three years there would be regular monorails to every one of the ten Daroks as well as to several outside research facilities. The Darok 10 Council knew what they were doing—Darok 10 had become the capital city of First Quadrant. Its people were wealthy with all of the business and tourism brought in by the multitude of travelers.

Maddie gasped. Hank realized that she had just spotted the station. He turned and waited for her to catch up. Her mouth gaped as she stared ahead at the enormous structure with elegant towers. He took her arm gently to keep her moving.

They turned onto Quasar. Finally, they were in military surroundings and he could breathe more easily. If Lydia were in Darok 10, she'd find it difficult getting into this district of the dome, although Hank knew she was quite capable of finding a way around the security. First Quadrant Headquarters dominated the entire street. In stark contrast to the elaborate station, its various buildings were built in a uniformly plain style with rectangular windows and flat roofs. The ComAp was at one end.

At the gate, Hank slid his security badge through the scanner. The guard directed him into a small booth at the side of the gate and asked him to step up to the retinal imager attached to the wall. Hank tried not to blink while his eyes were scanned. His heart quickened. Even though he knew he had clearance, he always feared that someday an imager would fail and he'd be denied access to a military establishment.

The guard smiled. "Thank you, Mr. Havard. Enjoy your new job here."

Hank smiled with relief. Now he hoped that Chris Conroy had already registered Maddie in the data base as a visitor so that she would be cleared as easily. She produced her Darok 9 ID card and handed it to the guard.

He nodded his approval.

"She's your responsibility, Mr. Havard," he warned as he handed Maddie her ID card.

"Okay," said Hank, putting his badge away and relaxing slightly. "Let's go and see Will's dad. He's in Apartment 5D."

Maddie pointed. "There's building D."

"There's only three floors with two apartments on each," said Hank, reading the numbers posted on the building. "Officers' luxury accommodation. My apartment will be small in comparison."

"Looks like 5 will be on the top floor," said Maddie, pointing to a sign on the wall.

"Great. That was easy. Now let's hope he's home and in a good mood."

"I don't think Captain Conroy's going to like what we've got to tell him, no matter what mood he's in," said Maddie.

"I know," agreed Hank. "He's got a temper, too."

"Let's hope Will is here."

Hank nodded. "It would be a great relief."

He braced himself as they approached the elevator, slid his security pass through the scanner and took a deep breath as he stepped inside. As brothers-in-law, he and Chris Conroy generally got along well. But any man would react angrily to the news that his wife was being held captive by Lydia Grant and his son was missing. Hank was not looking forward to being the bearer of bad news. The doors opened on the top floor and Hank led the way past apartment 6 to Chris's door. He knocked lightly.

"Who is it?"

"Hank."

The bolt immediately clicked back and the door opened. Captain Chris Conroy greeted them, his surprise evident.

"Hank! What are you doing here? Great to see you!" he exclaimed in his deep baritone voice. He grabbed Hank in a bear hug and patted him heartily on the back. "I thought you were arriving tomorrow afternoon. I was expecting Will and his friend . . ." He glanced at Maddie, apparently searching for her name.

"Maddie," she answered for him.

"Yes, I'm sorry, Maddie. We have met before." Chris's brows furrowed. "I thought you were coming with Will. Did I misunderstand in some way?"

"He's not here, then?" asked Maddie. She bit her lip.

Chris Conroy shook his head and looked at her with obvious confusion.

Hank could not keep silent any longer. It was time to break the bad news. "I think we'd better come in and tell you what's happened."

Chris suddenly looked worried. "Sure, come in...come in," he said, flustered. "Tell me what's happened...Will's okay, right?"

Hank didn't know where to begin. He watched Chris close the door. "I...I don't...I don't know," he stammered. "And I don't know quite how to say all this. You'd better sit down."

"Out with it, Hank. Just tell me if there's bad news!" Chris's voice rose. "What's happened to my boy?"

Maddie stepped forward. "Lydia Grant is what's happened!"

Hank cringed at her bluntness, but at least the bad news—or part of it—was out in the open. Maddie shrank back noticeably as soon as the words left her mouth.

Chris stared at her with a look of sheer horror. He turned to Hank, his brown eyes wide and bulging. "Is this true?"

Hank shuffled nervously from foot to foot. "Yeah, I'm afraid so. We think Lydia Grant abducted Will from the hopper port when he and Maddie arrived, but as yet we have no proof. We hoped he'd be here with you."

"Hang on a minute!" yelled Chris. "I'm obviously missing something! First, isn't that hideous woman dead? Second, what makes you think she has Will? The kids can't have arrived more than..." he looked at his watch. "Oh...is it *really* that time?"

"Yes, it's 1 a.m., Captain Conroy," said Maddie. "Will and I arrived in Darok 10 twenty minutes early—at 11:10—and then got separated."

"I apologize," Chris replied, his voice softening. He took Maddie's hands in his own. "I should have met you at the hopper port...shouldn't have been so stuck in my work. But Maddie, did you actually *see* Lydia Grant take Will?"

Maddie shook her head. "I think he and I must have

gone out different entrances."

Chris Conroy sighed. "Well, then. Aren't we all jumping to conclusions? I'm sure my son will find his way here any minute. I know Will—he's probably just got sidetracked."

"There's...there's more," said Hank, digging into his pocket. "This is why I'm so concerned about Will." He produced the crumpled note from Lydia and handed it to Chris, nervously waiting for his brother-in-law's reaction.

Chris slowly lowered himself onto the sofa. His eyes narrowed as he read the blackmail note. "Rachel ...not Rachel." He looked up at Hank with watery eyes. "You'd better begin at the beginning, Hank."

"Yes, of course," said Hank, wondering what was the beginning.

"And tell me *everything*," Chris added through gritted teeth.

"Would you like me to get you a glass of water, Captain Conroy?" Maddie interrupted.

Chris nodded, "Yes, thank you. I think I'm going to need it."

Maddie disappeared around the breakfast bar and Hank began to recount the tale, starting with Schumann's disappearance. Maddie returned with water just as he finished. Chris drank the entire glass, handed it back to her and said nothing.

"I blame myself," Hank found himself confessing in an effort to fill the awkward silence. He sat down next to Chris on the sofa and placed his head in his hands, rubbing his fingertips under his tired eyes. "I should have called Gillman at Darok 9 security force two days ago . . . but it never entered my mind that we were dealing with Lydia Grant until I got that letter. I was hesitant to get the security force involved because of what happened last year. Had I placed my trust in Darok 9 security force back then, Will would have died. If only I had contacted Gillman this time, maybe Rachel..."

Chris folded up the note, his mouth firmly set in a bitter expression. "Forget the 'if onlys' and the 'maybes,' Hank. It's too late for that!" He got to his feet and began to pace the floor in front of the sofa. "Regrets won't save Rachel—or Will, if Grant has him too. You're right—you should have involved the security force from the beginning. Come on, Hank, Gillman can be trusted—you know that. He stood by you last time we dealt with the mad woman and her cronies. You just enjoy playing amateur detective and once again my son and my wife are in danger."

"I love them like you do, Chris. I would never have involved them if I'd known that Lydia Grant was mixed up in all this, or if I'd thought that I was putting them in any real danger."

"That woman has threatened my family once too often," said Chris through clenched teeth. "This time she'll regret it. I'm calling First Quadrant Command immediately!"

Hank leaped to his feet. "You're making a big mistake, Chris. You read the letter. If we call the security force of either Darok 10 or Darok 9, Grant will kill Rachel."

"I'm *not* involving the security forces. I'm doing what I know best. I've got a team of military specialists at my disposal and I'm darn well going to use them!"

"If there's any involvement by *any* section of the military Lydia will kill Rachel and probably Will too," Hank pleaded.

Chris Conroy's face turned deep purple. "This is my call, Hank! They are *my* wife and *my* son. You put them at risk to begin with, so stay out of it from here!" He marched to the door and slammed it behind him.

Hank was stunned. He looked at Maddie. "That didn't go so well, did it?"

She shook her head.

Hank slumped down on the sofa and sighed heavily. "Why was I such an idiot? Chris was right—I was enjoying playing detective. I should have called Gillman."

Maddie sat down next to him. "You didn't know we were dealing with Lydia Grant, Mr. Havard. Will was enjoying this as much as you were...and so was I."

"Thanks, Maddie, for trying to make me feel better. But there's no excuse for my actions. I should have listened to Rachel."

"So what are we going to do now?" asked Maddie gently.

Hank turned to look at her. "I'm not sitting and waiting for Chris's special military team to spring into action, that's for sure. By the time he gets through all the red tape and convinces military command that there's a threat to the security of the Daroks and not just to his wife and kid, it'll be too late."

"I'm still game," said Maddie eagerly.

"I can't involve you anymore, Maddie," said Hank.

"Sorry, Mr. Havard, but I'm here to stay, so I suggest you count me in. I know Lydia Grant and what she's capable of. This is my choice. I know the risks. Will's my friend and I'm also to blame for his disappearance. I want to make amends just like you do."

Hank smiled to himself. He understood why Will liked Maddie so much—she was a gutsy young lady. And she was right, this was not something he could do on his own. "This is probably yet another bad decision I'm making, but you're in...and your help is welcome." He gave her a high five.

"Micky Rigby?" asked Maddie.

"Micky Rigby it is," replied Hank.

Chapter 11

Will opened his eyes to see Randolph Lazzar standing over him holding a steaming bowl. He leaped off the mattress, tripping over his own feet.

Lazzar laughed loudly out of the corner of his mouth. "Don't worry, I'm not about to tip anything over you. This is your breakfast." He placed the bowl down on the floor. "Miss Grant will be up to see you in a few minutes. If you know what's good for you, you'll treat her with respect this time."

After the door had closed Will sat back down on the makeshift bed. His heart was still racing. He picked up the bowl with both hands and sniffed the rising steam. He was ravenous. The sweet smell reminded him of a strawberry porridge that his mother often made. He dipped in the spoon and raised it to his lips, the tip of his tongue touching the delicious creamy mixture. He was about to put it into his mouth when a horrific thought crossed his mind. What if Lydia had drugged or poisoned the food?

Will placed the spoon back in the bowl and stared wistfully at the porridge. His stomach was rumbling, but he couldn't risk eating anything until he understood what Lydia wanted from him. It was unlikely she wanted him dead, or she would have killed him last night. But what if the porridge contained some kind of sleeping drug so he wouldn't put up a fight? The diabolical woman would have no qualms about doing that to him!

Will quickly carried the porridge into the bathroom, lifted the toilet lid and scraped the lumpy mixture into the toilet bowl. Water was scarce in the Daroks, and the trickle of toilet water barely carried the thick mixture away. When it had all been disposed of, he hurried back and placed the empty bowl on the floor by the mattress. He lay down on his stomach, buried his head in the pillow and closed his eyes. He had the perfect plan: he would feign sleep.

His heart raced as he waited for Lydia's arrival. Time seemed to pass slowly. Where was she? Even if the porridge weren't drugged, surely either she or Lazzar would check on him sometime. He lay still, listening for footsteps.

Time dragged, and pretending to sleep was not as easy as he had anticipated. Then he heard the door slowly open, and the sound of footsteps got louder and nearer—first light ones and then a heavier pair. Will recognized Lydia's voice as she and Lazzar whispered. He felt her presence...felt her breath as she leaned over him. He tried hard not to let his eyelids flutter, hardly dared to breathe, and forced his heart rate to slow. Someone prodded him in the side. Will had anticipated that and he managed to stifle his reflex. He was proud of himself that he hadn't reacted.

"He's out cold, Lydia. There'll be no trouble from him

for a few hours."

"Great, Lazzar. Watch him while I fetch Hank. Don't let anything happen to our bargaining chip."

"No worries. I can handle the brat."

"Good. It's already eight o'clock. If all goes according to plan I'll be back here by eleven with Hank, and we'll be on our way to Third Quadrant before anyone knows what has happened."

Will listened to the fading footsteps. His heart slowed. He strained to hear more of their conversation.

"What about the boy's mother and Schumann?"

Lydia laughed. "What about them? If someone finds them after we've left, lucky for them. If they die, too bad!"

The door closed.

Will exhaled deeply. He had been right. Thank goodness he knew what Lydia Grant was capable of. Her cold-blooded ruthlessness and disregard for human life was still difficult for him to comprehend. He remained still for a few minutes more, listening to the footsteps descending the stairs. Then he opened his eyes and sat up on the mattress. He was starving, but there was no time to think about that—he had to think of a way to escape. Time was precious. His uncle was about to meet with Lydia and Will was to be Lydia's bargaining chip—unless he could escape before Hank arrived. Besides, he had to find his mother and Doc Schumann. It was a tall order. His stomach churned. Every hour since Dr. Schumann's disappearance had brought more questions but still no answers. Was it already too late to save them?

Will tried to push that thought to the back of his mind. He looked around the room for a way out. Nothing came to mind. There were no other doors, no large air vents or pipes to the outside, and only one window, which had been boarded up with planks. Either he had to open the door and sneak past Lazzar or find a way to get through the window somehow.

Will removed his shoes and tiptoed to the door. Could they have left it open since they thought he had been drugged? His hopes were quickly dashed. It was locked *and* the bolt was electronic. He walked back to the window and examined the planks. They had been fastened with screws into the window frame. Will hoped that at this height, Lydia hadn't thought it necessary to install a security system—had she done so, there would be no way to get through the window without a decoder.

He needed something to undo the screws. Silently he slid open the desk drawers, but they were empty. He crawled on the floor looking for a flat, sharp object, thin enough to fit into the screw heads. Nothing. After ten minutes of searching he gave up.

He sat back down on the mattress feeling totally discouraged. There had to be a way out! His eyes fell on the porridge bowl. The spoon! Would it work as a screwdriver? It was certainly worth a try. His pulse quickened as he positioned the spoon edge into the head of a screw. The spoon was a little thick and the tip was curved, but he could just get enough leverage to turn the screw counter-clockwise. It moved just a fraction of an inch before it jarred in his hand and slipped from the slot. Will was frustrated, but he couldn't give up when his mother's life was at risk. *Patience, have patience,* he told himself. He steadied his hand and carefully positioned the spoon again. Yes! The screw turned through ninety degrees! Once again he repositioned the spoon and once again the screw turned.

Elated, he set to work. There were at least thirty screws to remove and time was short. He would need a steady hand and a great deal of patience, but he could do it. He prayed that Lazzar would not think to check on him for a while.

* * * * *

Maddie's watch alarm buzzed. She could barely open her eyes and yet her mind was already racing and her stomach cramping with both excitement and worry. Will! What had happened to him? She hoped he wasn't in any danger. Then she thought about Micky Rigby and her whole reason for coming to Darok 10. The stakes were high and she couldn't think about failure. The powerful daytime Darok 10 lights would soon be turned on, and she and Hank would put their plan into action.

She and Hank had stayed up until 3 a.m. discussing strategy. His passcode had enabled them to bring up plans and information about the entire Darok 10 military complex on his VisionCom. They had discovered that the new labs were located in Building C, the same building that housed the records department. Building C had been designed in an L shape, with the new labs occupying the first two floors and the records department in the basement. Maddie was nervous that their idea was so simple. She wished there had been a computer involved. Instead, their plan was like something pulled from the pages of a detective novel. How could it possibly work?

She leapt off the sofa and prodded Hank, still fast asleep in a living room chair, legs sprawled awkwardly over the arms. His small silver VisionCom was still turned on and lay open on his lap.

Hank stirred and his VisionCom fell on the floor. Half asleep, he reached over to pick it up.

"So, are we going to do it?" she asked, hardly waiting for him to open his eyes.

"I think we have to try," said Hank, stretching. "We don't have a lot of alternatives." He sat up and looked around the room. "No Will?"

Maddie shook her head and glanced at the clock. "No...no Will."

Hank took a deep breath. "I was hoping I'd been wrong. I wanted nothing more than to wake up this morning and see his face. Chris didn't return?"

Maddie shook her head a second time and mumbled, "Sorry, Mr. Havard."

"As I suspected," said Hank. "He'll spend the next twenty-four hours trying to cut through military red tape before he'll get anyone to do anything." He got to his feet and stretched his arms above his head. "If he can't convince the Supreme Commander of First Quadrant the Daroks are being threatened and not just his wife and son, the rescue will be left to the security force." He looked at his watch. "It's quarter to seven."

"We'd better get going. Only fifteen minutes until the cleaners finish their rounds and three hours until you have to be at the Galaxy Hotel to meet with Lydia."

"Okay. I'll make a quick visit to the bathroom—no time for a shower," said Hank, as he ran out of the room.

Maddie pulled on a clean top, slipped her sweatshirt back over her head and squeezed her dirty blouse into a side pocket on her pack. Hank returned to the living room a few minutes later. She grinned at him. "I'll be done in half the time it took you!"

Maddie ran to the bathroom, brushed her thick hair back into a ponytail and grimaced as she caught a glimpse of herself in the mirror. "You'll pass, Madeleine Goren. No time to be prissy today."

Hank was standing by the front door looking at his watch and grinning. "One minute, fifty-nine seconds. Not bad. Ready then?"

"But how will we get back into Captain Conroy's apartment?"

"I'm one step ahead of you for a change," said Hank. "I found a spare keycard in Chris's desk drawer late last night."

"Good news," said Maddie. She picked up her pack

and followed him out. They marched to the elevator and across Quasar Square. Within minutes they had reached the main doors of Building C. The guard on night duty stared at them through a large window beside the door.

"Please declare your business," he instructed though the intercom.

"Hank Havard, scientist, reporting for duty in the new labs. This is Madeleine Goren, a friend of Captain Chris Conroy. She has been registered as a visitor in your data base."

"Thank you, Mr. Havard. Both of you please step into the foyer and swipe your ID cards. I'll also need a retinal image from you, sir, and your bags will need to pass through the scanners."

Hank did as instructed, laying his briefcase on the rolling belt. Maddie swiped her Darok 9 ID card and placed her backpack next to Hank's case. She jumped when she heard two loud clunks. The inner doors slid open. The guard greeted them in the corridor and handed them their bags.

"Thank you, Mr. Havard. You're an early starter!" He held a small microphone to Hank's mouth. "Please state for the record what brings you into the building on a Sunday morning at seven."

"Miss Goren is only here for a short time and wanted to see the new science labs before she returns to Darok 9. I'm just giving her a quick guided tour to satisfy her curiosity. Captain Conroy has cleared her visit."

Maddie watched the guard's bemused face and decided to back up Hank's story. "I just *love* Darok 10," she said excitedly. "It's huge . . . and so far ahead of the technology in Darok 9. I can't wait to tell everyone back home what a neat place this is. I've got to catch a hopper in a couple of hours and I *desperately* wanted to see the new labs. I'm studying to be a scientist, you know. One day I'm..."

"That's fine, Miss Goren," said the guard, cutting her off in mid-sentence. He lowered the microphone and smiled. "I'm glad you are enjoying your stay so much. I promise that you won't be disappointed when you see the labs. I'm no scientist, but even I can appreciate the complexity of the equipment here." He looked out the front door, yawned and added, "Here's my replacement arriving. I'm off home to bed. You're entered in the register and have a maximum of one hour in the building. Check out with the new guard as you leave, please."

"We'll do that," said Hank.

Maddie looped her arm through Hank's as they walked away. "You have a good morning," she called back to the guard. Her heart quickened as they turned the corner and entered the main corridor. "That wasn't so hard, was it?" she whispered to Hank.

He smiled. "That's the easy part."

Maddie looked around in awe. The plain gray floors gleamed with newness under the bright lighting and the fresh paint on the walls was smooth and unmarked. The building even smelled new. Security cameras were everywhere, mounted on brackets suspended from the ceiling.

"So where's this fancy new lab?" she asked in a loud voice.

Hank steered her down the wide hallway. "Not far."

They paused outside a windowless door on the left. Hank ran his ID card through the slot in the door and ushered Maddie inside. "Pity my ID card won't get us into the records room," he whispered.

"It would have saved us a lot of trouble, for sure," said Maddie, stepping into the lab. She gasped, unable to take in everything she saw. A scientist of the future she was not, a computer expert—perhaps. The sheer scale of the computer equipment alone mesmerized her. High-speed delivery tubes connected various workstations around the room, and equipment, from small countertop apparatus to enormous free-standing machines, filled every available space. This room had equipment beyond her wildest dreams.

"Unbelievable," she exclaimed, looking up at the huge split-screens suspended from the ceiling. "Will you be working in here?"

"In here and in the adjoining lab," he replied, placing his briefcase on a countertop. He walked over to the connecting door between the two labs. "You can cut the act now, Maddie. There are no cameras in here because the research is top secret. You ready to go to work?"

Maddie nodded, although it was hard for her to take her eyes off her surroundings. "Sure. Okay, first we have to locate the cleaners' storage room in the basement. Do you remember from the plans which ventilation shaft in this room connects to it?"

"Right here," said Hank, bending down and pointing to a metal grid on the wall. "It's the one between the two labs." He tugged at the outside grid. "It's a little tight," he groaned, pulling until it finally gave way. He fell back on the floor, the grid on his chest.

"I don't think I'll be taking this," Maddie said, removing her backpack and passing it to Hank. She lay on her stomach and peered into the shiny silver shaft. She could see through to the lab next door. The shaft traveled horizontally for three feet across to the grid in the adjoining room, but in the middle another shaft plummeted down to the lower floor. "At least it's clean," she remarked.

"The building has only been open a few weeks so everything is still new," said Hank. "Now, according to the plans, the shaft will come out at the top of the basement wall. So you should only have to descend a few feet between this floor and the basement."

"I'll manage," said Maddie, already slithering into the shaft. "It's not much wider than my body so I can use my feet against the sides to break my fall."

"You know what to do once you get to the basement?"

Maddie nodded. "I've got to find the master passcard that the cleaners use to access the records room."

Hank looked at his watch. "It's now 7:09. The cleaners should be finished and gone from the building. I'll be here setting up my workstation...in case anyone decides to check on us."

Maddie crawled into the vent and positioned herself over the top of the downward shaft. "I can see the bottom, Mr. Havard."

"Okay. Good luck. Be as quick as you can."

Maddie lowered herself inch by inch, using her feet and her arms pressed hard against the sides to slow her descent. Although her thick sweatshirt cushioned her elbows, the shaft was so warm that she wished she had removed it.

Within minutes, her feet touched the bottom of the vent. She crouched down, unable to turn. She could see light shining through the grid but there was no way she could position herself in the narrow shaft to push at it.

"There's only one thing to do," she muttered. "I'll have to try and kick it off."

Maddie took a deep breath and kicked hard. The grid shook but remained steadfast. She tried again...and again...but the grid didn't budge. Now her clothes were sticking to her and the shaft felt even hotter and more claustophobic. She growled with frustration and tried again, wincing as she shoved her foot hard against the mesh. Finally, on the fifth attempt, the metal covering fell to the floor with a crash.

Maddie crouched down again and squeezed her legs through the hole. She winced as her right knee scraped the upper edge of the opening. Thank goodness she was wearing pants. Now she was sitting with her legs hanging down the wall. How would she get down to the floor? There was no room to twist around on her stomach. She would have to slither out on her back and she had no idea how far down it was to the floor.

She grabbed the metal frame of the grid and edged out of the shaft until her arms stretched above her head and her whole body hung down the wall. Her fingers slipped. She couldn't feel the floor. All she could do was let go and hope.

Maddie fell hard on her right foot. She stumbled forward on the cold stone floor and landed on her knees, stretching out her hands to steady her fall.

"Thank goodness it wasn't a huge drop," she muttered, clambering to her feet. She brushed off her hands and straightened her ponytail. She'd have some nice bruises in a few hours, but that was all.

Trying to ignore her throbbing knees, she surveyed the small room. The main light was on. Lockers stood against one wall and shelves of cleaning equipment were against the other three. Two benches were positioned in the middle of the room. Now where would cleaners keep a passcard? Well, when a cleaner finished his shift, he'd probably remove his coveralls and master passcard and store everything in a locker for the next day. Maddie worked her way along the row of lockers, pulling each handle. Frustration set in as one after another was locked. When finally she found three open lockers, she realized the futility of the plan. The open lockers contained no cleaning outfits and no master passcard, just jackets and shoes.

Maddie heard voices outside. Her heart beat furiously. It suddenly dawned on her—the three lockers contained street clothes and shoes, which meant that three cleaners were still in the building. She turned in circles. Where could she hide? Her gaze finally came to rest on the wide low benches in the middle of the room. There might just be enough room for her to squeeze underneath. As long as she kept still, she might get away with it.

The grid! It still lay on the floor where it had fallen! It was too late to put it back. Maddie hurriedly picked it up and shoved it in the corner between two shelving units. As she darted toward one of the benches, she said a silent prayer that the cleaners wouldn't look up and see the grid-less hole in the wall. She lay on her back and pulled herself underneath. The door opened and several people entered the room, chatting loudly. Maddie stared up at the dark brown underside of the bench, hardly daring to breathe. Her knees throbbed and her body ached. The cold stone floor sent chills through her clothes and up her back. She could not even look to see if her body was completely hidden.

The bench above her seemed to flex. Someone had sat down. Maddie turned her head to see a pair of female ankles in flat brown shoes positioned right next to her face. The owner bent over, undid the laces and removed the shoes. Maddie watched a green coverall slip down over the lady's ankles into a heap on the floor beside the bench. There was a light chinking noise. A white card on a long metal chain landed on top of the pile of clothing.

Maddie's heart skipped a beat. The white card looked remarkably like Hank's. It had to be a master passcard. If only she could reach it. The woman sitting on the bench stood up and walked over to the lockers. This was Maddie's chance. *Dare I?* she wondered.

She thrust her left hand out and groped until she felt the chain with her fingers. Could she pick it up without it jingling? Just then a locker handle rattled and the people in the room began laughing. She seized her opportunity and snatched the card up as the locker door clanged open. She gulped. Her heart pumped furiously. She waited for someone to shout and drag her out from underneath the bench, but the chatting and laughing continued. She clenched the chain tightly in her hand, praying that no one would notice the missing passcard.

The coveralls were picked up off the floor. There was more laughter and a short discussion about getting coffee in the staff lounge. The locker doors slammed shut and someone sat down on the bench again. Maddie watched the woman slip on a pair of black high-heeled shoes. Seconds later the door opened, the light was turned off and Maddie was alone again.

Maddie realized she was shaking. It took her several minutes to muster the courage to pull herself out from underneath the bench and find her way to the light switch. She uncurled her fingers. Her hand was imprinted with the marks of the metal chain that she had gripped so tightly. On the front of the card was the picture of a young, dark-haired lady, and on the back the familiar magnetic strip containing door codes. Maddie smiled and slipped the chain over her neck. "This has to be it. Mr. Havard will be delighted."

She looked up at the shaft entrance, high in the wall. How could she get back up the shaft to Mr. Havard? She and Will's uncle had not discussed this part of the plan! The bench wasn't tall enough, and there was nothing else in the room that she could climb on to reach the hole. She swallowed hard. She was stuck and time was running out. She had no choice but to look for Micky J. Rigby's records by herself.

Chapter 12

Will removed the final screw from the boarded window and placed the last slat of wood on the floor with the others. He tossed the screw up in the air and caught it with one hand. "Ha! Lydia Grant! Think you got me? Well, I'm out of here!"

He pushed on the upper edge of the window frame. It shifted slightly. He pushed again. With a huge jerk that almost sent his head through the glass, the bottom section moved upward, leaving a gaping hole.

He was exuberant. Freedom was but a short distance away. But as he peered through the open window he realized that his escape was not going to be as easy as he had thought. The drop to ground level was at least thirty feet, and without a fire escape or a rope, there was no way he could go down. He stared at the street below. It was very early on Sunday and not a soul was in sight. Should he scream for help? If no one but Lazzar heard his cries all his efforts would be wasted. He had to get out while he had the chance.

Holding tightly to the frame, Will sat on the windowsill, his back out the window and his feet inside the room. He leaned back and looked up. Down the side of the window every fourth row of bricks jutted out several inches.

"Yes!" he said excitedly. This simple design feature of

the building would be his ticket to freedom. He felt sure that he could find his footing and climb the eight feet from the windowsill to the flat roof. Once on the roof, he could walk along the roof to the nearest fire escape.

"You can do it, Will," he muttered, as he carefully pulled himself to a standing position on the sill. His knees wobbled and his pulse quickened. He fought to keep his fingers curled around the top of the window frame. They slipped slightly, but he dug his fingernails in determinedly and inched sideways toward the brickwork.

He heard an angry shout from inside. His blood pounded in his ears. Randolph Lazzar must have entered the room and seen the open window. Will reached for the brick above his head and struggled to find his footing. He reached up a second time and hauled himself up another foot. Just as he reached up for the third brick jutting out, a hand grabbed his ankle. Will gasped. He tried to shake his leg free but the fingers tightened their grip. He froze. Any sudden movement and he'd slip and fall.

"Going somewhere?" hissed Lazzar.

Will didn't reply. He looked up. The roof was only a foot above his hand. If only he could reach the fancy trim that jutted out from the edge of the roofline.

"Do I pull you off that ledge and probably to your death, or are you coming back in without a fuss?"

"I don't think Miss Grant would approve of you killing her bargaining chip, do you?" asked Will, trying to buy time.

"Miss Grant wouldn't approve of you escaping, either," replied Lazzar. "What's it to be, boy?"

"Okay, okay," said Will. "Just let go of my ankle—you're hurting me."

Lazzar let go of Will's ankle and extended his arm to Will. "Now get down from there and make it snappy!"

Will looked him in the eyes and started to bend down as though he were about to grab Lazzar's hand. Then in one quick movement he lunged for the roof molding, groaning as his arms took his full body weight and his legs dangled beneath him. His heart raced. He focused on the roof above and struggled to pull his feet out of Lazzar's reach, his shoes scraping on the wall as he desperately tried to push himself up. He found his footing on the bricks, scaled the wall and heaved himself onto the rooftop.

"You brat!" Lazzar hollered. "I'll get you—you little..."

The roof seemed to flex under his weight. Will gulped. In his desperation to escape he'd forgotten that Darok roofs were not built to be load-bearing—they were only for appearance and to contain noise. The main Darok dome provided protection from the extreme lunar environment.

Will lay perfectly still. His mind raced. He couldn't stay where he was. Could he make it to the nearest fire escape without the roof caving in under his weight?

Carefully, he got to his feet and began to tread lightly along the edge of the roof, figuring that had to be one of the strongest parts. He swallowed hard and tried not to look down. Walking so close to the edge was frightening. If he fell, that would be the end of him. Concentrating on the black metal rails of the fire escape jutting above the roof, he carefully placed one foot in front of the other.

"Ten feet to go," he muttered. "Just ten more feet."

Lazzar's scarred face suddenly popped up at the top of the fire escape. Shocked, Will staggered backward, nearly losing his balance. Lydia's henchman blocked his route to the ground.

"There's no escape, boy," Lazzar grinned. "Give up before you get hurt."

Will looked around. How could he escape? A hundred feet of roof expanse lay between him and the fire escape on the far side of the building. The roof had supported his weight so far, but would it continue to?

Lazzar, seething, scrambled up the ladder and stood at the top.

"You'll have to catch me first," Will taunted.

Lazzar growled and stepped onto the roof.

It was now or never. Will turned and ran. He heard Lazzar's heavy footsteps close behind. The man was actually coming after him! He felt the roof shake with the additional weight and movement. Will's stomach was in knots as he reached the middle. Surely the flimsy roof couldn't support both of them. He looked for the rivets that fastened the roof to the supporting central beam, and followed them across the expanse to the edge and the fire escape.

The roof groaned. There was an almighty crack.

Lazzar yelled. Will looked back to see his pursuer stuck, one foot caught in a hole in the roof.

Will grinned. He lunged for the handrail to the fire escape, threw himself over the edge, and slid down to the top step of the ladder. He started down the fire escape, hardly able to contain his relief and his glee. Mr. Randolph Lazzar would be very busy for a while.

* * * * *

Maddie opened the door of the tiny cleaning room and peered out into the hallway. She listened for a few seconds. Convinced that no one was about, she poked her head into the basement corridor. Security cameras were everywhere. She ducked back inside the room.

"Drat! Now what, Madeleine?" she mumbled in frustration. "How are you going to get into the records room without being seen?"

Simply...she wasn't. As soon as she left the cleaning room she'd be seen on the monitors. The cameras were too high to smash or cover—and what good would that do anyway? The guard would be down here in an instant to investigate. There had to be another way. She dropped onto the bench and sighed. Her eyes wandered to the shelves in the corner. Cleaners' outfits! Laundered, folded and ready to go. If the guard saw a cleaner going into the records room, he'd think nothing of it. Or would he? Maddie looked at her watch. It was now 7:15. The cleaners were supposed to finish at seven, but they were late today and had talked about getting a coffee before leaving. Perhaps the guard would think nothing of a worker staying late. It was worth a try.

Maddie took the top coverall off the pile, unbuttoned the front and pulled the garment over her pants and sweatshirt. *My ponytail—it's a giveaway*, she thought, undoing the rubber band and allowing her hair to fall over her shoulders. She dragged a cart stacked with cleaning supplies from the corner of the room. Drawing a deep breath, Maddie opened the door and pushed the cart determinedly into the corridor.

It was only a few feet across the corridor to the double doors that led to the records room. Keeping her head down, Maddie lifted the master passcard hanging around her neck and swiped it through the slot. A buzzer sounded and the door bolt clicked open. *What ingenuity, Madeleine Goren!* She felt a rush of excitement at her success as she wheeled the cleaning cart into the records room, away from the cameras.

Once inside, Maddie stood with her back against the closed door and sighed with relief. The low-ceilinged room was filled with row after row of tall shelving units containing neatly labeled files. Where would she find files beginning with 'R'? As she looked across the room, wondering where to begin her search, she caught her breath. A large camera was angled directly at her. Maddie's heart pounded. Hank had said the labs had no inside cameras because of the sensitive work that went on inside. Stupidly she had assumed that meant the other rooms wouldn't have cameras either. Maddie hurriedly grabbed a duster and a bottle of cleaning solution from the cart and began to squirt shelves, polishing furiously as she went along the rows, standing on her tip-toes to reach the top. Occasionally she paused and looked at the files. At least they were labeled alphabetically.

But after five minutes of frantic cleaning, Maddie was dejected. She had only reached row 'E', and now she had to continue her careful cleaning. If a guard were observing her activities at the front desk, she had to appear to be working systematically. Cleaners did not skip rows.

Maddie rounded the end of another aisle and quickly glanced at her watch. Fifteen minutes had now passed since she'd entered the records room. Would the guard see through her disguise? She dismissed the thought and concentrated on the files on the middle shelf. *'P'...nearly there. Don't get too enthusiastic,* she told herself. *Must keep working at the same pace.*

When she finally saw the first file beginning with an 'R', she could hardly contain her excitement. Her heart pumped furiously and her hands trembled as she moved methodically along the row. She read the files on the upper shelf—Ra, Radkin, Radson, Rawling—and then those on the middle shelf—Re, Reed, Reston, Reynolds—and squatted down to look at the bottom shelf—Rider, Rifkin, RIGBY! She couldn't believe her luck. There it was, staring right at her: Micky J. Rigby.

She turned her back to the camera at the end of the row and in one quick motion, unzipped her coveralls. Then, as she continued to dust with her left hand, she removed the file from the shelf with her right, squeezed the fat folder into her coverall and zipped it up again.

Maddie realized that she was sweating profusely. Had she gotten away with it? She looked at her watch. Forty-five minutes had elapsed since she'd entered the building, although it felt like hours. Time was running out. The hour was almost up and Mr. Havard would be worried.

Maddie headed to the door, put the cleaning equipment back on the cart and wheeled it into the corridor. Now what? She couldn't get back up the shaft in the cleaner's room. She would have to leave in a more traditional way. Her gaze fell on the elevator at the end of the corridor. She whistled as she hurriedly pushed the cart toward it and pressed the button.

Maddie maneuvered the cart inside. After the doors closed, she peeled off the coveralls and tucked the file under her sweatshirt. When the doors reopened on the ground floor she abandoned the cart and walked out of the elevator with her arms wrapped tightly around her middle. She drew a deep breath as she approached the laboratory door and raised her hand to knock.

"Miss Goren," said a deep voice behind her. "Where is Mr. Havard?"

Maddie's heart skipped a beat. As she turned to face

the guard, she clenched her teeth and contorted her face into what she hoped was a pained expression. "He's still in the lab sorting out his new workstation. I...um...had to visit the bathroom."

"Are you feeling okay?" asked the guard looking down at her arms.

Maddie bent over, clutched her stomach and groaned loudly. "I seem to have developed stomach cramps. It's good that we're leaving soon."

"Indeed it is," remarked the guard, swiping his pass through the slot and opening the lab door for her. "I suggest you tell Mr. Havard about your stomach problems immediately."

Maddie nodded and groaned again.

The guard's VisionCom beeped. He pulled it from his belt and flipped it open. "I'm sorry, but I'm needed at the entrance. Don't forget to check out when you leave," he reminded Maddie as he walked away.

Hank ran down the lab to meet her, his face pale and brow furrowed. "Are you okay? I've been out of my mind with worry."

Maddie closed the door, stood upright and pulled the file from under her sweatshirt. "I'm fine now," she replied with a smile, "but this took some doing."

Hank took the file from her and held it as though it were a precious stone, his face erupting into a broad grin. "Micky J. Rigby's file. You're amazing, Maddie," he said, putting it quickly in his briefcase. "Let's get out of here—fast. You can tell me how you did it—later."

"Oh, by the way..." said Maddie, as they walked to the door. "I'll have serious stomach cramps in about thirty seconds."

Hank looked confused. "You'll have what?"

"Just play along and we'll be fine," said Maddie, groaning and doubling over as he closed the lab door after them. "I need to get home fast, right?"

"Got it," said Hank, helping her down the corridor.

Chapter 13

Hank flew through the door of Chris Conroy's apartment and eagerly took out the fat file from his briefcase. He marched to the back of the open-plan living area where Maddie helped him spread out the papers on the dining room table.

Hank sorted the information on Micky J. Rigby into two piles: personal information and research. "You take the personal information. We've less than two hours before I have to meet Lydia, and I'd like some clue as to what she's after before I see her."

Maddie pulled out a chair and picked up the first sheet of paper. She laughed. "Well, here's something we got wrong, for starters."

"What?" asked Hank, still staring at the paper in his own hands.

"Micky J. Rigby is a *she,* not a he!"

"Really?" Hank looked up.

"Born Michaela Jayne in 2079 and died, age 39, in 2118. Her husband, Tom Rigby, is still alive, and she has no security force record. Seems as if she was a model lunar citizen. The body was transferred immediately to Darok 9 on March 4, 2118 and cryopreserved the same day. She's in tank 2, cylinder 15."

Hank began to pace. "So, Rachel was right. Michaela

Jayne is a Darok 9 cryopatient."

"Oh, my goodness! Look at this!" Maddie shrieked.

"What?" asked Hank, dashing to her side.

"Michaela was Gunter Schumann's younger sister!"

Hank felt hot. He took the paper from Maddie and looked at the paragraph headed 'Family Information.' Now they were getting somewhere. "This *has* to be important," he mumbled. "Gunter must have information about his sister that Lydia wants."

"And if we can find out what it is we'll solve everything," said Maddie, her voice high with excitement.

"Very simply put," said Hank with a groan. "Though I've a feeling it's not going to be that easy."

Maddie seemed undeterred. "So where do we start?" she asked enthusiastically.

Hank picked up the thicker pile of papers and wandered over to the living room sofa. "I'll look at the research documents. You continue reading about her life," he said with a sigh.

He sat down and forced himself to scan the pages of data, flipping through the papers and stopping when something caught his interest. Michaela had been an eminent molecular robotics scientist in Darok 2. Her research had won her many awards. It seemed that Michaela had been looking for new ways to maintain a safe lunar environment for humans living on the Moon—a controlled climate and a consistent supply of water.

"Hmm," said Hank. "It has to be something to do with her research. I just need to find out what she was working on when she died." He rushed back to the table. "When she died," he repeated slowly. He grabbed Maddie's pile of papers. "Her death!" he shouted. "Quick! What did she die from? Where's that information?"

"Third page," said Maddie.

"Accidental death," he read aloud and then silently read the rest.

"Well?" asked Maddie after a few minutes. "What does it say?"

"In plain and simple words Michaela Rigby died of head injuries caused by a fall in the molecular science labs."

"I can tell you don't believe it," said Maddie instantly.

Hank shook his head. "You bet I don't. How many people fall in our labs? They have so many safety rules. And then to die? This whole thing smells of a cover-up."

Maddie's jaw dropped. "You think she was murdered?"

Hank raised his eyebrows. "I didn't say that...but it's easy to jump to that conclusion. Mighty suspicious, don't you think?" He handed her the pile of papers and wandered back to the living room to retrieve the others. "There's something missing, but I just don't know what. Maybe she was murdered because of the research she was doing."

"Well, read to me what's written down," said Maddie, twisting around in the chair to look at him.

Hank flipped back to the third page. "Okay, special projects. She received several four-year grants from the First Quadrant Life Research Organization. The first was in 2106 and the last in 2114. Then in 2118 she was given a large grant from First Quadrant military. Doesn't say much else..."

"Stop!" shouted Maddie. "You're overlooking the obvious!"

"I am?" questioned Hank. "Enlighten me, quickly."

"You said in 2118 she was given a large grant from the First Quadrant military. Michaela died in 2118. Don't you find it odd that the project that Michaela was working on the year she died was funded by the military when all the others were funded by the Life Research Organization?"

Hank nodded. "So it was...and therefore the research was probably of a more sensitive nature."

"Does it say what the project was about?"

"It just says *Molecular Robotics and Liquid Crystal*," said Hank, raising his eyebrows. "That's an odd combination."

Hank felt the blood drain from his face. He stared at Maddie and slowly lowered the papers to his lap. He'd just figured out what Lydia was up to. "No!" he bellowed. "The Daroks could be destroyed. The whole population of First Quadrant could be at risk!"

Maddie stared at him. "I don't get it. What do molecular robotics and liquid crystals have to do with the population of First Quadrant? What *is* molecular robotics?"

"Robotic computers so small that they are invisible to the human eye. Molecular robotics has been researched for over a century. Before the disaster on Earth, scientists were developing the idea of using them during human surgery. It's taken us another hundred years to get back to where they left off on Earth."

"So what's the connection with liquid crystals?"

"You know that a thin film of liquid crystal is sandwiched between the silicon-based layers that form our Darok domes."

Maddie nodded.

"Michaela Rigby may have learned how to program robots to eat their way through the molecules in the liquid crystal. Since they're invisible to the naked eye, the microscopic robots could destroy the domes before anyone realized they were even there."

"Without the dome for protection, we'd all die," said Maddie, her voice quaking.

"And what better way to eliminate an entire Quadrant in one sweep than to put the domes out of action?"

"But why would Michaela work on something so destructive that no good could come of it? You're not suggesting she was another Lydia Grant, are you?"

"No," said Hank adamantly. "Michaela's research probably began with the intent of finding a way to maintain the structure of the domes. It is a known fact that the liquid crystals in the domes deteriorate with age and will eventually have to be replaced. I'll bet that Micky Rigby was researching how molecular robots could be used to perform maintenance work, or perhaps strengthen and rebuild the liquid crystal or even the silicon layers of the domes."

"You think that Lydia Grant found out what Micky Rigby was doing and saw how her research could be used to destroy the Daroks?"

"That would be my guess," said Hank. "Lydia Grant or someone who knew Lydia Grant."

"But Michaela Rigby is dead. If there had been any memory cards or notes about her research, wouldn't those have been in the records department with everything else we found?"

"You'd think so," said Hank, concentrating hard.

"Could someone have taken over the robotic research when she died?"

"Unlikely. I know how the military works. Most of us don't have access to other scientists' research for security reasons. Just like with my SH33 project last year—only two other people knew what I was working on and no one but Lydia, who was my assistant at the time, knew how far I had come with the research. Sure, I had notes on memory cards, but a large part of my work was in my head. When scientists die, a lot of their research often dies with them."

"Now there's an idea. Did Michaela have an assistant?"

Hank flipped through the file. "Sorry. There's no mention of anyone."

"There goes another good theory," said Maddie.

"'Fraid so."

"So how would Lydia Grant get detailed research from a dead person?"

"That's what we have to figure out," said Hank, wagging his finger in the air. He glanced at the time. "It's nearly ten o'clock. I have to meet Lydia. There's no way I'm going to be late for *this* meeting."

"Shall I come with you?"

Hank smiled. "Thanks, Maddie, but no. The note said to come to the Galaxy Hotel alone and I must do that or I'll put Rachel at risk. Lydia Grant will do exactly what she's threatened to do if I don't follow her instructions."

"So what should I do while you're gone?"

"Wait here and keep looking through the file. If I'm not back by noon, contact Richard Gillman in Darok 9, tell him about Rachel and get him to send out a search party. He knows you can be trusted so he'll listen to you."

"What about the file? Do I hide it when I'm done?"

Hank shook his head. "I'm taking responsibility—I don't want you in trouble. The security force will figure it out sooner or later anyway."

"Then I'll give the file to Captain Conroy. He'll understand that I took it to save his family," said Maddie, handing Hank his briefcase.

"*You* took it to save his family? I thought we had just agreed . . . *I* took it to save his family."

Maddie grinned, her face reddening. "Okay...you win."

Hank waved goodbye, closed the apartment door and set off down the stairs. "Once again I'm trying to save the entire First Quadrant as well as my family," he muttered under his breath. "How do I get myself into these situations?"

* * * * *

Will turned in frantic circles at the end of Jupiter. He glanced over his shoulder. There was no sign of Lazzar. He was torn over what to do next. Lydia had already left to meet his uncle and Will didn't know where. So should he make his way to his dad's apartment at the ComAp or should he try to find his mom? Decisions! He hated them—and there was so much at stake!

Lydia's words replayed in his mind over and over again. *'Your mother will die a long and painful death in Darok 9.'* What had that evil woman done with his mother?

"Darok 9!" he shouted. "She said Darok 9!" Lydia had unwittingly given him a clue.

The hopper port was just a short distance down Saturn—he could leave Darok 10 in search of his mother before Lydia Grant realized he was missing. The ComAp, on the other hand, could be a mile away or more, and it was where his enemies would assume he'd run, so they might just catch up with him before he made it. Besides, his mom's life was in danger. His gut told him he had to get home. Decision made. He could call his father later, perhaps even with good news about his mother, but for now he had to get safely away from here.

Will bent to pick up his pack. His stomach knotted with panic. Where was his pack? It was still in the room where he had been held prisoner! That meant he had no ration cards or ID card, and he wouldn't be able to buy a ticket back to Darok 9 or call anyone. The decision had been made for him. "Now I've got to go to the ComAp," he said glumly.

His heart sank. He had no idea how to get there and he'd be taking a risk walking through the streets. Lazzar was probably off the roof and already looking for him. But he had no choice.

Will quickly walked away from the hopper port, keeping close to the buildings. He kept his head down and shoved his hands in his pant pockets as he strode along the sidewalk. His fingers rubbed up against something square and thick in his pocket. Then he felt a long thin piece of plastic. A rush of excitement consumed him. He knew what it was without even looking—his ID card and return ticket to Darok 9 were still in his pocket! In his hurry to board the hopper last night he had not put them back in his wallet.

Without hesitation, Will turned and ran down the street to the hopper port, ignoring the honking zoomers and the few pedestrians who had ventured out early on a Sunday morning. The powerful Darok lights, dim less than an hour before, were now glaringly bright.

Will ran through the hopper port entrance to the check-in desk and laid his ticket in front of the old man behind the counter. Breathlessly he asked, "How long before the next hopper to Darok 9?"

"If you get a move-on, sonny, there's one in five minutes," he said, checking Will's identification. "Gate 4."

Will tore along the moving walkway, up the ramp and into the waiting craft, checking over his shoulder one last time for signs of his captors. He slid into the first seat, slouched down so that no one would see him, and stared through the windows, frantically scouring the gate and boarding ramp. Still no sign of Lydia or Lazzar.

The hopper doors closed and his heart pounded. Only a few minutes more and he would be safe. When the engines started, overpowering relief swept over him. He took a deep breath and settled back into his chair. A smile crept across his lips when he visualized Lazzar with his foot stuck through the roof. He chuckled to himself.

As Will watched the bright lights of the Darok 10 dome fade from view, his heart suddenly sank. Gunter Schumann and his mother had been kidnapped, he had no idea what had happened to Maddie, and he still knew nothing about Micky Rigby. Why was he celebrating when the whole trip to Darok 10 had been a complete and utter disaster?

Chapter 14

Hank signed the guest register, which lay open on the front desk of the Galaxy Hotel. He took the key and the code to room 36 from the concierge, and walked quickly along the carpeted hallway of the west wing. At any other time he would have stopped to admire the handcrafted furniture in the window bays, the realistic silk plants and the elaborate décor so uncommon in the Daroks. But today he was filled with so much anger and worry that it was all he could do to read the numbers stenciled on the doors.

He felt uneasy as he passed room 34. The next room on the right was his destination. Would Lydia be waiting for him or would she make a dramatic entrance after ten o'clock? Hank paused to look at his watch. He had fifteen minutes to spare.

His fingers trembled as he inserted the key into the lock and punched in the four-digit code. He had hoped that he would never have to see Lydia Grant again. The woman was pure evil. But once again he had no choice but to follow her instructions and he had only himself to blame for the situation he was in.

The door swung open. Hank swallowed hard, took a deep breath and boldly entered. He stood inside the open doorway scanning the room. There was no sign of Lydia. He relaxed slightly, closed the door and walked around, examining everything in the room. He had never stayed in a hotel. None of the other Daroks had one. Visitors to Darok 9 had to stay with family or friends or in army quarters. He wondered if that might change now that Darok 10 had led the way. Perhaps Darok 9 would soon have a hotel.

The hotel room was just as he had imagined a hotel room might look: small and square and attractively decorated. The room was crammed with a bed, dresser, chair and desk, leaving a small walkway around the bed. A door next to the desk led to an ensuite bathroom. He guessed that was all one needed for a night's stay.

Hank walked over to the window and drew back the pale yellow curtains. If he looked through the window at an angle, he could just see Saturn Avenue and the canopy over the main entrance of the hotel. He wondered if there was only one entrance to the Galaxy. Would he be able to see Lydia arrive from here?

Hank dragged the heavy ornate chair across the room to the window and propped the curtain back with the desk lamp so that he could see the street below. He sat down, looked at his watch and waited. A few minutes passed. His hands felt clammy and the collar on his shirt felt tight. He undid the top button and looked out the window a second time. More minutes passed. Hank shifted his position, looked at his watch again, and waited some more. By ten minutes after ten, Hank was irritated and his shirt wet with perspiration. Was the whole thing a ploy to get him away from Darok 9 as Maddie had suggested?

The VisionCom on the desk buzzed. Hank leaped off the chair and pressed the *'accept call'* button. "Lydia?" he shouted.

Expecting to see Lydia's curly dark hair, he was shocked when Lydia's face, framed by short red hair, appeared on the screen.

"My dear Hank."

"Lydia?" asked Hank, taken aback by her new appearance.

"I can see by your expression that you like my red hair."

Hank snorted and said nothing.

"I am so pleased to see that you followed instructions and came by yourself," she continued in a patronizing tone.

"But of course," replied Hank. "Do you think I would risk Rachel's life?"

"I'm glad you remembered that I don't play games. Your nephew will also be pleased that you had the good sense to take me seriously."

Hank's heart sank. "You *do* have Will, then."

Lydia laughed harshly. Her wide mouth stretched into a taut smile. "But of course, Hank. I'm always one step ahead of you—you should know that!"

She laughed again, throwing back her head as he had seen her do thousands of times before—only now she had no curly black hair to toss over her shoulders.

"What do you want of me, Lydia?" he demanded.

The hypnotic centers of her eyes seemed to pull him toward the screen.

"Your help," she replied tersely.

"What makes you think I'll help you?" said Hank, trying to put up some kind of resistance.

"Because if you don't, you will never see Rachel or Will again!" she screamed, thrusting her face forward. "Surely that's enough!"

"Okay," said Hank, shrugging his shoulders in resignation. "What do you want me to do?"

"That's better," replied Lydia as if she were talking to a child. "Leave the Galaxy Hotel and walk down Saturn. I'll be watching you every step of the way. Go to the VisionCom booth set into the wall outside The Stargazer Restaurant."

"And then?" asked Hank.

Her eyes gleamed with malice. "And then you'll get further instructions."

"How do I know that you really have Will and Rachel?"

"My dear Hank. You know me better than that. You'll get proof."

"You hurt either of them, Lydia, and you'll have no help from me. Do I make myself clear?" Hank shouted.

"*You* are in *no* position to bargain with me, Hank!" Lydia spat. "Now do what I've asked!"

The screen went blank. Hank realized he was shaking—more out of anger than fear. How could he have allowed this diabolical woman to threaten his family again? This time Lydia would know what to expect from him and it wouldn't be as easy to fool her.

As Hank headed down the corridor to the front desk, he took out his Com and dialed Chris Conroy's apartment. He'd decided to keep Maddie informed every step of the way so that someone would know where he was.

Her youthful face broke into a smile the instant she answered his call. "Mr. Havard, I've been so worried. Are you okay? Did you see Lydia Grant? Has she got Will?"

Hank tried to be brief but reassuring. "I'm fine, Maddie. Lydia is sending me somewhere else before she shows herself. I guess she's checking I'm not being followed. I'll stay in touch."

He handed his key to the clerk and tucked the Com into his pocket as he left the hotel.

Hank had gone less than a block when he spotted The Stargazer Restaurant across the street. He crossed quickly, his spine tingling at the thought that Lydia was somewhere close by. He approached the screen and waited. Anger rose in his stomach as the minutes ticked by and the screen remained blank.

The gray screen suddenly flashed blue. A high-pitched buzzer sounded, and Lydia's face confronted him once again. She laughed loudly before speaking.

"Good, Hank. I am pleased to see that you are listening to me," she said in a condescending tone. "Let's hope you continue to do so."

Hank's patience was waning. "Just get on with it, Lydia," he snapped. "I don't have time for this!"

"Be careful, Hank," Lydia shot back, her expression turning from a relaxed smile to a stony stare. She wagged her finger at him. "You'd better remember who's running the show. Make the time!"

Hank's blood boiled. This woman didn't deserve any respect and yet he could do nothing but follow her demands. He didn't reply to her rebuke but pasted a neutral expression on his face.

"That's better, Hank," she said, her wide smile returning. "You will walk down Saturn to Jupiter Circle. At the end of Jupiter you will see a three-story building with a sign that says, 'Lazzar Technologies.' I'll be waiting inside."

Hank looked down Saturn. He could see the side street from where he was standing. "I'm on my way."

"Oh, and Hank . . . drop your VisionCom into the trash can next to you before you go any farther. We don't want you calling anyone, now do we?" The screen went blank.

Hank sighed. He removed the Com from his pocket and held it for a second above the bin. A chill ran down his spine. He bit his lip and glanced across the street. How close was Lydia? Would she see if he made one last call to Maddie or if he slipped the Com back into his pocket? His heart raced and his palms felt clammy. He hesitated and then dismissed the idea. Rachel and Will's lives were on the line and Lydia was a formidable opponent. She'd search him for a Com before he entered the building even if she couldn't see what he was doing at that moment. He had to think through this situation carefully and not make rash decisions. He drew in a deep breath, opened his hand and watched the Com fall into the trash.

Now he was on his own.

Hank set off down the street at a brisk pace, turned the corner onto Jupiter Circle, and within minutes came to a brass plaque inscribed *Lazzar Technologies*.

"Lazzar," he muttered to himself. "Where have I heard that name before?" He couldn't quite place it. He approached the door and wondered whether to knock.

As if in answer to his question, the door opened. A tall man with a scarred face, a weapon slung over his shoulder, stood before him. "In here," he grunted.

Hank stepped through the doorway expecting to see Lydia. His heart sank when he saw nothing but an empty entrance hall. Would he be given another set of instructions and sent on his way a third time?

The door by the stairs slowly opened and Lydia entered. She stood in the doorway, thrust her hands in the front pockets of her pants, tossed back her head and smiled wickedly. The temperature of the room seemed to suddenly drop as she strode toward him. Hank studied her flared pants and flat shoes. Not the Lydia he knew. He shuddered. The woman looked more sinister in casual clothing than she did in a white lab coat.

"Lydia," he muttered, not knowing whether to be happy that he had finally caught up with her or angry that the evil woman was standing before him.

"What's the matter, Hank?" she said with a laugh. "Can't quite believe it, can you? I suspect that you were hoping that this was all some kind of hoax and that your precious SH33 had killed me long ago."

"I can't deny that I never wanted to lay eyes on you again," Hank said. "And I can't understand how you have no remorse or guilt, or how you'd even dare come back here!"

"Hank...Hank...as steadfast in your beliefs as ever. Always so good, so moral. For you, everything is black or white, wrong or right. There are no shades of gray." Her smile turned upside down and she thrust out her chin in a haughty manner. "Well, life just isn't that simple!" she spat. "Where I failed last time, I will succeed this time. If you believe in something you follow it through to the end. You, Darok 9's most eminent scientist, should know that!"

Hank was seething. He could control his anger no longer. "How dare you compare my dedication to my scientific research, for the good of mankind, to..." He was lost for words. "To...this!"

Lydia smiled. "What's the matter, Hank? Can't quite say it? Kidnapping!"

"How about murder?" Hank shot back.

Lydia laughed harshly. She stepped up to him, scraped the long nail of her index finger across his cheek, and whispered silkily in his ear, "Not yet."

"Gunter Schumann's alive?"

"Last time I saw him," she replied coolly, throwing a

glance at the man with a scar.

Hank gulped. "And Rachel?...and Will?"

"For now it suits my purpose to keep them alive. That is, as long as you cooperate."

"I want proof you have them!" Hank demanded.

Lydia nodded at her colleague, who gave her his laser and bounded up the stairs two at a time. Lydia aimed it at Hank. "Step back," she ordered, balancing the weapon with her right hand while delving into a pocket with her left. She tossed Hank a small black VisionCom. "This is your sister's."

Hank flipped up the lid and studied the call log. His hands shook as he read the list of calls his sister had made and received. He played the messages that Will had left for her. His stomach tightened. There was no denying it. The Com was Rachel's.

The disfigured man returned and dropped a deep blue backpack at Hank's feet. "The boy's," he grunted.

Hank looked up to see Lydia smirking with satisfaction.

"I think you have your proof," she said without emotion.

Hank clenched his fists and screamed at her. "What have you done with them? Is Will here...in this building? Let me see him! Immediately!"

Lydia handed the laser back to the scarred man, who stood watching Hank's every move. "My dear Hank, normally so controlled. You'll see young Mr. Conroy when I get what *I* want."

"Not good enough. How do I know that you didn't just steal Will's backpack and Rachel's phone?"

"Oh, Hank, really! You know me better than that."

"I want *real* proof, Lydia!"

"Run the security program," Lydia ordered her colleague. "And Hank, this is all you're going to get." She motioned to a small monitor attached to the ceiling. "If you look up at the screen, you will see that the security cameras filmed young Mr. Conroy arriving here just a few hours ago."

Hank watched the videotape of Will entering the building, and saw his nephew's horrorstruck expression as Lydia peeled off her disguise. He felt ill. "No more. I've seen enough. Turn it off."

"I can see I have made my point," said Lydia with obvious satisfaction.

"Indeed you have. So let's get *to* the point. What do you want from me?"

"I'll show you," Lydia replied curtly, leading him through the door to the right of the stairs.

Hank followed in silence, his mind racing. The moment Hank entered the room he knew the answer. Against the far wall was a large brown table on which sat the latest optical computer, a retinal scanner and a small device that he instantly recognized as a microchip decoder.

He gasped. "You've got Micky Rigby's research!"

"I guessed that you would eventually work out my connection with Micky Rigby," said Lydia, her black eyes sharpening. "I tried to warn you off, Hank, but you and your family had to stick your noses in. If it hadn't been for your meddling sister you might never have known that I was even in Darok 9. But, as it happens, I need your help, so your interference has worked to my advantage."

"But—but how? How did you get her research?" Hank stammered. "Micky Rigby's been cryopreserved! Oh, my goodness! You didn't find a way to...did you?"

A look of disbelief crossed Lydia's face. "Find a way to bring her back to life? Is that what you were going to say?" She threw back her head and cackled. "Really, Hank! As if I could! What do I know about cryopreservation techniques?" She turned and smiled at him in a knowing way.

Hank stiffened. "But there weren't any memory card records of her research in the First Quadrant records department. Her work was classified."

"You *have* been busy," said Lydia in a tone that awarded Hank a certain amount of admiration. "But then I would expect nothing less from you, Hank."

"So how did you get hold of her work?"

Lydia tossed back her head and laughed loudly and uncontrollably. "Not difficult. I'm sorry, I haven't yet introduced you." She gestured to the scarred man who was walking back into the room. "Meet Randolph Lazzar, eminent military forensic scientist, originally from Darok 2." The man pulled his scarred face into a tight smile.

"Of course. Lazzar," said Hank. "I knew I'd heard the name. But no one had access to the details of Micky Rigby's research. I know that from the records...and I know how the military works. Only a senior military advisor would have understood the full implications of her research and how far along she was."

"Indeed," said Lydia, showing satisfaction at Hank's bewilderment. "But Micky and Lazzar were research cases in their own right and good friends because of it."

"I don't follow," said Hank.

Lazzar touched the laser to his forehead and ran the tip along the length of his scar. "See this?" he said curtly.

Hank nodded. How could he not?

"That's First Quadrant military for you!" said Lazzar with obvious bitterness. "Micky and I were test cases. We each had a device implanted in our brains that recorded on a microchip all of our thoughts and research as we worked. Hers functioned well for several years. Mine...well, let's just say that it immediately became dislodged and I was lucky to survive." He tapped his forehead. "This is the result of two years in a coma and twelve operations to reconstruct my face and repair my brain."

Hank shuddered. He couldn't take his eyes off the ugly scar, which went all the way across Lazzar's forehead, well below his hairline. "I heard rumors of such microchip research, but never imagined it had been tested."

Lydia opened the decoder and removed a translucent microchip, which she twirled in her fingers in front of Hank's face. "Micky worked on a very sensitive project. When she died, this very powerful microchip, containing all of the research she had gathered during the project, was surgically removed before she was cryogenically frozen."

"And let me guess," interrupted Hank, finally putting the pieces together. "You turned Gunter Schumann's apartment upside down to find it since he was her brother and he also performs the cryonics."

"Bravo!" Lydia clapped her hands three times slowly. "Almost right, Hank. But Gunter didn't have it. When we established that it wasn't in his apartment we had to think again. The microchip had been placed in Micky Rigby's box in the Darok 9 Cryolab safe. Box number 15 to be precise. Only Gunter, your sister and Commander Gillman have entry codes. It wouldn't have been difficult to break the safe code, but I did it without even trying. You sister can be so stupid. Fancy selecting S-H-3-3 for her code. Everyone in Darok 9 could have guessed that!"

Hank decided to ignore the insult to Rachel and continued with his questions. "I presume, Lazzar, that you knew what Micky was working on even if you didn't know how far she had progressed," continued Hank.

Lazzar pressed the tip of the laser into Hank's chest. "I've waited patiently for years for this moment," he snarled. "My life was taken away from me by a government more concerned with research than with the scientists working for them."

"So you murdered her," said Hank.

Lazzar's mouth twisted into a half-smile. "I didn't have to. Micky tripped in the lab."

Hank shook his head. "Don't believe it. No one trips

in our labs with all their safety rules and regulations, and certainly no one dies from such a fall."

"They do if a microchip planted in their brain dislodges and causes a seizure," Lazzar countered.

Hank gasped at the revelation. He could not deny that everything he was being told fit the facts. "And then the First Quadrant military hushed up the true cause of her death—the seizure—to hide the failure of the microchip research," concluded Hank.

"Accidental death due to a fall," said Lazzar. "She even had the cracked skull for the records. No messy investigation."

Hank looked Lazzar in the eyes. "And now you want revenge?"

"Dead right," replied Lazzar. "Lydia and I—and Micky—we all suffered at the hands of First Quadrant military. This is my second chance at life."

"By doing what?" asked Hank.

Lydia's smile broadened. "We are going to download the information on the microchip and use it for our own good in the United Quadrants." There was a lethal calmness in her voice.

Hank glowered at her. "And then you will use Micky's research to destroy the Daroks."

Lydia looked surprised a second time. "I take it that you know what she had discovered?"

"She was studying how molecular robots could be used to repair and preserve the Darok domes. I can only conclude that what molecular robots can repair they can also destroy."

"Correct, as always, my dear Hank."

"So why am I here? What do I know of molecular robotics? You know that my scientific field is completely different. I work with chemicals, formulae and equations. There's no way I can interpret the information stored on this microchip. I wouldn't know one end of a molecular robot from the other."

"I am well aware of that. But that's *not* why you are here or what I want from you, Hank."

"Then what?"

"Lazzar Technologies has been created for a reason. By setting up these forensic labs with the support of The Darok 10 New Enterprise Committee I can now link with the First Quadrant Net without any questions asked. But to download the information from the microchip I need to obtain the project code, which is stored on the First Quadrant military data base."

Hank sighed. "I'm not a computer hacker, Lydia."

"You don't need to be. To get into that data base all I need are two passcodes and matching retinal scans of military employees who have security clearance. One employee must have a clearance of Level 2 or above and the second person must be at least a Level 4. Lazzar works for the security force and therefore has clearance at Level 2..."

"And let me guess," said Hank sarcastically. "You need me because your clearance was deleted after you turned against First Quadrant and became a security risk."

"Correct again. You are Level 5 and a good bet, wouldn't you say?"

"I won't do this, Lydia. I *won't* help you."

Her expression immediately changed to a stony glare. "You have no choice!"

"I do. I won't give you my code and the power to destroy thousands of lives in order to save my family."

"Admirable, my dear Hank...but not sensible. I have the chip. If you won't help, I'll find someone else who will. You're expendable, brilliant scientist or not. Everyone is." She gave a dismissive wave. "There are other military personnel who have Level 4 clearance. It will only be a matter of time before someone else will help me—someone just as disillusioned as I am by First Quadrant practices. So why not save your family while you can? A life in the United Quadrants could be good for a scientist like you."

Hank tried to keep calm. "And why should I trust you? What guarantee do I have that you won't kill me and my family anyway?"

"My word," replied Lydia quickly.

"Ah! Your word," he repeated. "Your word is worth nothing. And what of the thousands you'll kill in First Quadrant when the Daroks are destroyed by these molecular robots? How will *I* live with that?"

She turned her back to Hank. "I'm not out to destroy the Daroks. I'm out for a position on the United Quadrants' government. This is my ticket to the prestige and honor and respect that I have always deserved." She swung around and flashed the chip in front of his face. "When one government holds a weapon of mass destruction, they don't have to use it to get what they want. The *threat* of its existence is enough. I'll leave you to think about it for an hour." Lydia, the chip clenched tightly in her hand, thrust her fist at Hank and marched out with Lazzar on her heels.

Hank fell into the chair in front of the computer. What should he do? If he helped Lydia, he could endanger the entire population of First Quadrant. She would have the power to hold the First Quadrant to ransom or to destroy it within hours. But if he didn't help her, Lydia would kill Rachel, Will—and him.

Worst of all, he knew she was right. If he didn't cooperate, Lydia would simply find another military scientist, driven by greed, revenge or power, who would.

The only way to save the Daroks was to destroy the microchip and with it, Micky Rigby's research. He had to find a way.

Chapter 15

Will drummed his fingers impatiently against the window frame as the hopper pulled up to the dock in Darok 9. He was out of his seat and down the aisle before any other passenger had moved.

"Thanks," he shouted to the attendant as he flew through the doors and leaped onto the moving walkway. He ran along, overtaking everyone else. There was only one thing on his mind—finding his mother.

Will tore across the lobby and out into Aldrin Court. He stopped for a moment, shocked at the small size of the Darok 9 dome compared with the enormity of Darok 10—it barely cleared the tops of the buildings. But this was not the time for contemplation or comparison.

He raced across the cobbled streets to the hospital, through the revolving doors, and up to the clerk at the check-in desk.

"Jerry," said Will, gasping. "Have you seen my mom?"

"Not today," Jerry replied, looking up from his book. He raised one wiry eyebrow and gave Will a confused expression. "It's two o'clock on Sunday, Will. Isn't she at home?"

Will shook his head. "I haven't seen her since yesterday. She came back to the hospital to do some research. It would have been mid-afternoon—around three o'clock."

Jerry looked concerned. "Let me check the computer log. I wasn't on duty yesterday."

"Well?" said Will, straining to read the screen.

"It appears she checked in at 3:10 and didn't sign out."

"I knew it!" said Will, slamming his hands down on the desk. "Call Darok 9 security force—Commander Richard Gillman. Ask him to get over here immediately!"

"But, Will..."

"Just tell him I need his help," he yelled as he ran to the elevator. "Tell him that Lydia Grant is back. He'll come."

Through the closing elevator doors, Will saw Jerry dive for his VisionCom. His heart raced furiously as he descended to the basement. Anger welled up inside him. If Lydia Grant had hurt his mother, he'd...he'd... he didn't know what he would do.

"Please, let her be okay," he prayed over and over again.

The elevator doors opened. Will raced down the corridor and through the double doors of the Pathology Department. The room was eerily quiet. After a moment's hesitation, he turned on the lights, scouring the room quickly. There was no sign of anyone. His mind raced. What was he thinking? Lydia Grant wouldn't have left his mother in plain view of the door. Perhaps she was tied up in Dr. Schumann's office?

He ran across the room and peered through the

window that partitioned off the tiny office from the main room. The desk lamp was on.

"Mom? Mom, are you there?" he called, edging his way around to the door. Swallowing his fear, he entered the little room. "Mom, are you in here? Are you okay?"

His heart raced as he moved to the desk and peered behind. There was no sign of his mother and the computer was still on. *Where could she be? The filing room!* His mom had mentioned she would file the folders in the room out back on Monday.

Will ran back into the Pathology Department and threw open the door to the filing room. He turned on the light and stared at the rows of cabinets. Nothing. His heart sank. Where else could he look?

A cold feeling passed over him. *A long and painful death*, Lydia had said. His stomach knotted. "Please, no!" he shouted out.

He found himself walking into the corridor and staring at the door to the Cryolab. Surely Lydia Grant wouldn't have done something so horrible as to put his mother and Gunter Schumann in one of the cryotanks. As much as he liked cryonics, he couldn't bear such a ghastly thought! But then, Lydia had no compassion. He had to get inside the Cryolab and see for himself.

Will stared at the keypad on the wall. He had watched his mother punch in her code on Friday night. It was a sequence of four digits or letters, but he had no clue what they were. *What would she have chosen? Knowing Mom, it would be something she could easily remember.*

Her birthday, perhaps? No, too easy. His birthday?

Will pursed his lips and tried entering his birth date, October 1st. That would be 1001. His hands shook as he punched in the digits, but the light on the pad still flashed red. *How about the year he was born?* He keyed in 2107 but still there was no change in the red light. He felt his frustration rise. His hands were clammy and his head pounded. *Come on, Will, what would Mom use as her code? Their house number, 104A, perhaps? No, that was way too easy for someone to figure out.*

Will slammed his hand against the wall in anger just as the elevator doors opened. He turned to see the heavy figure of Commander Gillman, dressed in a dark green military uniform, step into the corridor. Major John Wells, tall and lanky, and Mackenzie Stewart, his uncle's friend, followed closely behind.

Relief consumed him. He took a deep breath and muttered, "Thank goodness you're here."

"Will, what's going on?" Gillman asked in his bass voice. "Mac had just told me about Gunter Schumann's disappearance when Jerry called and said that your mother has also gone missing. And more disturbing, he mentioned Lydia Grant."

"Thanks for coming right away, Commander Gillman," said Will. "I don't really know where to begin, but I guess Mr. Stewart has told you a lot of it already."

Gillman scratched his beard. "It sounds as though there's a lot more I haven't heard! Start with your mother."

The tears that Will had been stifling for hours crept into the corners of his eyes. "I went to Darok 10 to visit my dad, but when I got there Lydia Grant and her goon grabbed me and locked me up. She told me that my mother was being held captive back here in Darok 9 and that she would die a long and painful death."

Gillman's eyebrows shot up. "Hang on there. You've actually *seen* Lydia Grant?"

Will nodded. He bit his bottom lip to keep it from quivering. "She's alive and as evil as ever. I've no idea what she's up to but I'm really frightened for my mom. I think Lydia Grant may have put her in..." He swallowed hard. "...in one of the cryotanks!"

"Let's get this door open!" bellowed Gillman.

"I've been trying but I don't know Mom's code."

Gillman reached for the pad. "I do—and I hold the master code. Your mom's code is SH33, the name of your Uncle Hank's miracle drug."

Will sighed. Why hadn't he thought of that?

The light turned green and Gillman opened the door to the Cryolab. "I think you'd better stay here," he said, putting out his hand to prevent Will from entering. "Mac, remain with Will. John, let's take a look."

"*Please*, I've got to help my mother," said Will, trying to push past Gillman.

Will felt Mac's strong hands grab hold of his arm. "It's best you stay with me," he said softly. "The Commander will let us know if your mother is inside."

Will could hardly contain himself. His head spun and

his legs wobbled as though they would collapse at any moment. He waited impatiently for several minutes, but finally could stand it no longer. "Is she there?" he asked with a shaky voice.

"No, she's not," replied Gillman without emotion. "You can come in now."

Will slowly entered the Cryolab and circled each tank, checking every tube carefully. He had to see for himself. The last three containers were still empty, just as they had been on Friday. He sighed with relief.

Gillman placed his hand on Will's shoulder. "Are you okay?" he asked.

Will nodded. "I've got to call my dad. He has no idea about Mom and he'll be worried sick about me."

"No problem," replied Gillman quietly. "We'll get your father here by military jet as soon as possible. Major Wells, get on that right now, will you?"

Will swallowed hard. "I was hoping to have good news for him. I didn't want to have to tell him about Mom and Lydia Grant because he'll blame Uncle Hank. I know Uncle Hank had a meeting with Lydia Grant, but I don't know if he's okay, and I've got to find Maddie—we got separated in Darok 10. I hope Lazzar didn't kidnap her, too."

"Lazzar," repeated Gillman. "That name sounds familiar. This is Lydia's goon, as you called him?"

Will nodded.

Mac was suddenly beside them. "Describe this man to me, Will."

"Horrible man. He has a scar right across his forehead like you wouldn't believe!"

"That's not the Lazzar who works in forensics with you, is it, Mac?" asked Gillman.

"One and the same. Randolph Lazzar."

Gillman's eyebrows raised in surprise. "Wasn't he reassigned from the Darok 2 labs?"

Mac nodded. "He's been in the department about eighteen months. Had some major surgery not long ago but never said why. Told me he was looking for a new start after his recovery and decided to come to Darok 9. The Darok 10 New Enterprise Committee recently gave him funds to set up his own forensic labs over there. He travels to Darok 10 just about every weekend."

"If Lazzar's working with Grant, what's the bet that his new labs are just a cover for something more sinister?" suggested Gillman. He turned to Will. "Do you remember where this place is?"

"Sure," replied Will, picturing the building. "It's not a place I'll ever forget. It's at the end of Jupiter Circle."

"Good," said Gillman. "We'll get Darok 10 security force involved."

Mac sighed. "Well, that probably explains how I ended up in hospital. Lazzar was still in the labs late on Friday when I arrived with the blood and hair samples from the hospital carpet. He offered to help me test them so that I could get home."

"And you think he drugged you somehow?" asked Will.

"Seems like the most plausible suggestion right now,"

agreed Mac. "We had a drink in the staff lounge while we were waiting for the test results. By the time I got home I didn't feel well."

"Okay. That's enough for now," said Commander Gillman in a reassuring voice. "The pieces are beginning to come together. Let's go back to my office. We'll sit down and Will can tell me the whole story."

Will looked at Gillman's smiling face. He knew the Commander was doing his best to offer reassurance, but things couldn't be more desperate. "I've got to find Mom," he begged.

"We'll see what we can figure out," replied Gillman.

Will grabbed his arm. "But time's running out, sir. We have to find her immediately. You know what Lydia Grant is capable of!"

"Don't worry...we're not going to waste time," said Gillman. "We'll form a search plan based on what we know of Grant, her activities and movements. All military maneuvers need a strategy. And Will, you look ill. When did you last eat?"

Will sighed. He'd been so worried his stomach was in knots, and he didn't feel like eating. But the Commander was right. He hadn't eaten since his snack on the hopper with Maddie. His stomach had been rumbling for hours. "Yesterday," he muttered.

"That settles it, then," said Gillman, with obvious satisfaction. "You can eat while we strategize, and I promise we'll find your mom."

* * * * *

Hank rubbed his eyes as he sat in front of the microchip decoder. The last two days had been a nightmare. He was exhausted. As he scratched his chin absentmindedly it dawned on him that he hadn't shaved since Friday morning. He hadn't slept much since Friday morning, either. He yawned sleepily. Just when he should have his wits about him he could barely keep his eyes open. He was sure Lydia would return at any minute and he'd have to give her an answer. Was he prepared to help her carry out her devious plan?

He stood up, shook his limbs and rotated his head in an effort to ease his stiff neck. "Come on, Hank. Get it together," he muttered to himself. "What's the matter with you? Stay awake and think clearly!"

The woman was insane and her intelligence made her insanity even more dangerous. But what Lydia thought was a well laid-out plan had serious flaws. Did she really think that the United Quadrants would allow the Daroks to remain? United Quadrants had destroyed Darok 9's water supply last year and would certainly obliterate the Daroks if given the opportunity. It was more likely that Lydia knew that, but didn't care as long as she got what she wanted out of the deal.

Hank growled in anger. Even if United Quadrants did nothing with Micky Rigby's research and used it only as a threat, the First Quadrant military would take no chances. Hank knew how the commanders planned for every scenario. They would be likely to wipe out all of the United Quadrants' lunar colonies to prevent such an attack on the Daroks from ever happening. This would be the beginning of a major lunar war! Would anyone survive? Once again Earth's checkered history was repeating itself on the Moon.

Hank got to his feet and paced back and forth in front of the decoder. He was beginning to think that his involvement in this whole sordid affair did have a positive side. Had he not discovered what Lydia was up to, some other scientist probably would have helped her. At least he had the opportunity to stop her. Lydia was intelligent, but he had outsmarted the woman before and could surely do it again. "I *will* find a way," he said with determination, pounding his fist into the palm of his left hand. But just as quickly as his confidence had spiraled upward, it plummeted. This was fighting talk, but he had no idea how he would defeat Lydia Grant.

Hank looked around the empty room. "Lazzar Technologies," he muttered. It seemed odd. Lydia had said that Lazzar Technologies had been created to give her access to the First Quadrant Net. But why go to so much trouble? Lazzar worked in the Darok 9 forensic labs. Lydia could have easily hacked into that system and made her escape to the United Quadrants. As it was, she had been walking around undetected in Darok 9 for several days.

Unless...

Hank's stomach turned. Darok 10 was the capital city

of the First Quadrant and the largest, most advanced Darok. What better way to secure herself a position in the United Quadrants' government than to destroy the First Quadrant's showpiece of technology?

Hank boiled. He didn't know whether he was angrier with Lydia or with himself. He'd been so naïve! Lydia was lying. She did have *every* intention of destroying a Darok and killing thousands of people in the process. What better place to launch a devastating attack than from inside the enemy's home?

Hank could see it all clearly in his mind. Lydia was patient. She would take her time to slowly and covertly bring in the needed equipment and robotics scientists, all under the guise of Lazzar Technologies. Then she would strike when no one expected.

Hank shuddered. He knew he had stumbled on the truth. Once Lydia had what she wanted she would kill everyone who knew her secret—Rachel, Will, Gunter and Hank himself.

The door opened and Lydia swept into the room. Lazzar remained at the door, laser trained on Hank.

Hank's adrenaline kicked in and his tiredness seemed to dissolve. He needed to stall for time while he figured out how to destroy the microchip. The fate of the entire population of the Moon was in his hands.

"Well?" Lydia demanded, eyeing him with a calculating expression. "What have you decided?"

Hank gritted his teeth. He drew himself tall and spat out, "Okay."

Lydia seemed to relax. Her smile broadened. "I knew you'd see sense," she gloated. "So let's get to work."

"The chip?" asked Hank.

"Right here," she responded, dropping it into the decoder. "Lazzar will give you his passcode and provide his retinal image when you get that far."

"I need something to eat first," said Hank. "We've time—and I refuse to do anything on an empty stomach."

Lydia's mood changed sharply. "You wouldn't be stalling, would you, Hank? Time is what you don't have!" She looked at her watch. "I'd say that your sister and Gunter Schumann have only enough water for another day."

Hank swung around in the chair. "What have you done with them, Lydia? Where are they? I swear, I'll..."

Her eyes burned into him. "You'll do nothing but work, Hank. Every minute is precious. Remember that! And don't think you can trick me. I want to see the thousands of pages of research downloading in front of my eyes. Then I want the data stored and copied onto memory cards as a backup before I give it to United Quadrant scientists. I don't care if it takes all night and a hundred memory cards! And I'd better be able to see it happening."

Hank sighed. He swiveled back to face the computer and mumbled, "Okay. Let's access the Moon Net."

Lydia hovered over him. Hank could feel her hot breath on the back of his neck. He tapped into the system, trying to ignore her presence. Within seconds he had reached the gateway to First Quadrant military and had found the project code data base. It was all happening too fast and too easily and there was nothing he could do about it.

Hank turned his head to look at Lazzar. Could he somehow cause a diversion to get Lazzar out of the room? Then perhaps he could overpower Lydia. Lazzar caught his glance and walked forward, positioning himself at Hank's side and aiming the laser at Hank's head. It was as if Lazzar had read his mind. Hank felt completely helpless.

"Retinal image number 1 now required," instructed the computer.

Lazzar stepped up close to the scanner on the side of the computer, keeping the laser aimed at Hank, his finger firmly on the trigger.

Hank knew it was now or never. Lazzar was distracted and Lydia had no weapon. He pushed himself from his chair and lunged at Lazzar, yelling loudly as he tackled him.

As Lazzar fell backward, the laser launched from his hands. Lydia screamed. Hank watched the laser fly across the room and dived for it as it fell, but Lydia snatched the weapon off the floor as he reached for it.

"Nice try, Hank," she spat, waving the laser at him. "But that's your last chance. Try that again and I'll kill you instantly. Now sit back down."

Hank sat reluctantly back at the computer.

Lazzar picked himself off the floor and threw himself at

Hank, snarling as his fingers wrapped around Hank's neck. "I'll kill you before I let you lay a finger on me again!"

He could hear Lydia shouting, "Lazzar! Stop!" But Lazzar tightened his grip around Hank's throat, pressing into his windpipe. Hank gasped for air.

Hank struggled to pry open his attacker's fingers, but he couldn't fight off the man. He began to choke. He couldn't breathe!

"Lazzar! Come to your senses!" shouted Lydia. "I said stop this! We need him alive for now. You can kill him with pleasure if he doesn't cooperate."

Hank gulped in air as the fingers loosened. It was difficult to swallow. He massaged his sore neck muscles, gasping for air. His attempt had been worth the effort, but he probably wouldn't have a second opportunity since Lydia would be watching him more closely.

"You stupid man!" hissed Lydia at her colleague.

Without a response, Lazzar moved back in front of the scanner. A bright light flashed and the computer acknowledged the image of his eye.

"Now you, Hank," said Lydia, her mouth still twisted in anger.

Hank was trapped. It was too late. If he delayed any longer Lydia would kill him for refusing to cooperate.

He hesitated.

"Now, Hank!" Lydia screamed.

Hank reluctantly looked into the tiny eye piece and waited for the flash of light.

Lazzar typed his passcode into the computer and then prodded Hank in the back. "Your turn," he snarled.

With shaking hands Hank entered his eight-digit military passcode.

"Access approved," announced the computer. *"State research scientist name."*

"Micky Rigby," said Hank, quietly.

"Project code 2-7A-82-4632. Enter project code into microchip decoder and begin download."

Hank drew in a deep breath.

The screen remained blank.

"Type in the project code again," snapped Lydia. "You must have done something wrong."

Hank repeated the exercise, calling out the sequence number by number.

The screen remained blank.

"Do it again!" Lydia screamed.

Hank keyed the numbers again. When still nothing appeared on the screen he stood up and turned to face Lydia. His spirits were soaring. Trying to contain his laughter, he announced, "There's no research! You've got yourself a completely blank microchip!" Then he erupted into fits of laughter.

Lydia turned a vivid scarlet and whacked Hank across the face with the laser. "You're lying, Hank!"

Hank stumbled sideways and raised his hand to his stinging cheek. In spite of the pain he could not help but delight in her angry response. His cheek was wet. He looked at his fingers and saw they were covered in blood.

But he didn't care. His prayers had been answered for now.

Lazzar peered at the screen. "What went wrong? This is definitely the microchip from box 15. *I* took it out of the box!"

"This *is* Micky Rigby's research!" spat Lydia. "What did you do, Hank?"

"Fix it!" Lazzar bellowed.

"I didn't do anything. It's blank, I tell you!" Hank felt a stream of blood roll down his cheek and drip from his chin. "I don't doubt that Lazzar took the chip from her box, but there's no research on liquid crystal repair, molecular robotics...or anything else! Look for yourself!"

Lydia's embarrassment turned to raw fury. She pointed it at Hank's face. "That bloody cheek is just a taste of my anger, Hank. If you've wiped the data off somehow, you're dead right now!"

Hank wiped the smirk off his face, fearing that Lydia might lose control. He looked her straight in the eye and said as calmly as he could, "Now how could I have done that, Lydia? You watched every move I made. I did only what I was instructed."

Her black eyes opened wide. "Gunter Schumann," she growled. "How dare he! He's the only one who could have switched the microchips." She waved the laser around. Then suddenly she seemed to calm. She turned to Hank, her expression still thunderous. "Rigby was Schumann's sister. *He* performed the operation to remove the chip before she was frozen. I'll bet he switched the microchips and still has the original." A chill hung on her words.

Hank stared at her. What would Lydia do now?

"We're taking a Bullet ride," she said, as if she had heard his thoughts.

"To Darok 9?" asked Hank, already knowing the answer.

Lydia's eyes narrowed. "Just remember that Lazzar will be here watching Will."

Lazzar's mouth twisted into a menacing grin.

Hank's anger rose. "I want to see Will before we go. I have cooperated this far. Surely you can grant me that much, Lydia."

From the expression on her face, Hank thought Lydia was about to approve his request, but then Lazzar cut in.

"You'll get nothing," he snapped. "You'll see the boy when the goods are delivered and not a moment before."

Lydia seemed taken aback by her colleague's decision. Hank saw her throw an uneasy look in Lazzar's direction. She turned to Hank, composed herself for a minute, and said, "Exactly. You deliver and then we'll deliver. That's the deal. The boy's fine where he is."

Hank wasn't sure what he had just witnessed, but something didn't seem quite right between Lydia and Lazzar.

"I'll be checking in with Lazzar every hour," continued Lydia. "You pull any kind of stunt on the journey back to Darok 9 and your precious nephew will be dead before you can make a Com call. What's more, you will never find your sister in time to save her. She will die a painful and lonely death if she doesn't go mad first! Do I make myself clear?"

"As always, Lydia," said Hank with resignation. "Can I at least clean the blood off my face first?"

"Take him to the washroom," she ordered Lazzar. "Find him some gauze."

Hank grunted his acknowledgment and tried to hide his joy. This was his first gleam of hope in two days so now was not the time to upset her. At least Lydia had confirmed that Rachel was still alive. And since Gunter was the only one who knew where Micky Rigby's last research had been hidden, if Lydia was taking him back to Darok 9, it could mean only one thing—Gunter Schumann was also still alive.

Chapter 16

"**D**o you hear that, Gunter?" Rachel muttered.

"What?"

"Someone's out there," she said, staggering to her feet and pressing her left ear to the door.

"You're just imagining it," mumbled Gunter. "This room is soundproof. Sit down and don't exert yourself. There's no water left."

"I'm sure I heard voices," Rachel insisted. She rubbed her arms vigorously in an effort to keep warm.

"Wishful thinking," replied Gunter. "The voices are in your head. Unless Grant had an attack of conscience and returned to free us—and I doubt that." He snorted.

Rachel put her ear to the door a second time. Gunter was right. It *was* wishful thinking. The cryosafe was soundproof—they couldn't hear anything outside and no one could hear their cries for help either. But she was positive that Will and Hank were looking for her. And she was sure that by now, twenty-four hours after her nightmare began, the whole of Darok 9 security force had to be on alert. She was determined to keep her spirits up.

She leaned against the door and stared at the rows of open boxes on the opposite wall. She and Gunter had amused themselves for hours going through the personal effects of the cryopatients. Now that every box had been opened and there was nothing left to do, it was getting harder to remain positive. Time ticked slowly by. The boredom had set in and the confining space and chilly air heightened her despair. Surely someone would put the pieces together and realize where they were! Pieces? What pieces?

"Gunter," said Rachel, kneeling down next to him. "Please help me understand why I'm here...what *we're* doing here."

"What good will it do you, Rachel?" snapped Gunter. "The less you know the better—I've told you that."

Rachel's anger rose. Perhaps it was the confined space. Perhaps it was her fading hope. But suddenly her temper flared. "Because you *owe* me that much, Gunter!" she shouted. "Go on . . . satisfy my curiosity! If I'm going to die in this box with you at least tell me why! Why is Lydia Grant back? What is she after this time? And why does it involve you and Micky Rigby?"

She watched Gunter's gaze drop to the music box still clasped firmly in his hands. He stiffened and pursed his lips, but remained silent.

Rachel's annoyance surged at his stubbornness. Clenching her teeth, she snatched the music box from his hands and scrambled to her feet. "Give me the key!" she shouted, holding the music box above her head. "If you don't, I'll smash your precious music box to smithereens right here, right now!"

Gunter gasped. His nostrils flared with fury and he glared at her with burning eyes. "No, please...don't...don't do that." He ferreted in his pocket, breathing heavily. His hands shook as he held out the key, dangling from its thin red ribbon.

Rachel grabbed the key, jammed it into the lock and turned it clockwise as far as it would go. As she lifted the lid of the box the music played and the ballerina rotated. "Tell me, Gunter!" she screamed. "Is it the tune? Is there some kind of hidden message in the melody? Why is this old thing so important? And don't try and tell me that it's got sentimental value!"

Gunter looked bewildered. "It does, actually. It *really* was my great-great-grandmother's. There's no message in the tune. The box is just my connection to all the family I've ever had. I'm an old man with nothing but my memories. So please...don't..."

"Gunter!" Rachel hissed. "Tell me why we're in here! Tell me about Micky Rigby or I swear I'll..."

"Okay, okay. I've had enough," sighed Gunter, raising his hand in resignation. He muttered slowly and uneasily, "Micky was my sister."

"Your sister?" repeated Rachel, almost choking on the words. This was the last thing she'd expected him to say.

Gunter nodded. "Micky was my sister and she loved that music box."

Rachel lowered the lid of the music box and moved backward until she was as far from Gunter as she could get. She stood staring at him, shocked by what he had just revealed.

"I don't understand," she finally said. "Micky J. Rigby,

the woman frozen in tank 2, is...is your sister?"

"It's a long story," said Gunter, his voice filled with anguish.

"Well, we've got plenty of time and nothing else to do," said Rachel, sliding down the wall to sit on the floor. Gently, she set the music box down beside her and pushed it away. "Please, Gunter. Tell me."

Gunter sighed. "As you wish. Micky was a brilliant molecular robotics scientist working on a classified project in Darok 2. She was also one of two participants in a First Quadrant human research project that went wrong."

Rachel felt a terrible tenseness in her body. She could not take her eyes away from Gunter's pained expression.

He took a deep breath and continued. "She had a microchip implanted in her brain that recorded all of her work on how we could use robotics to repair the Darok domes. The microchip became dislodged, causing her to have a seizure. She volunteered to be a human test case, but it ended her life."

Rachel heard herself gasp. "I'm so sorry, Gunter. I never would have imagined..."

"I know. It's a terrible tragedy. Of course when the human microchip research failed *and* caused her death it was immediately hushed up by the military. Her death was recorded as a fall in the lab—accidental death. As a concession to me, and more probably to keep me quiet, they agreed to let Micky take up a place in one of the cryotanks."

"So, how does this all connect you with Lydia Grant?"

Gunter laughed. "I brought this on myself."

"I don't follow."

"I should have let Micky be, but I didn't. When I found out about the microchip implant I was angry . . . very angry. Then all I could think about was the great waste of her brilliant mind and how her research would never be used for the good of human survival on the Moon. So..." Gunter paused and looked Rachel squarely in the eyes.

"So?" asked Rachel, her body tensing as she waited for the end of the story.

"So I removed the microchip before placing her in cylinder 15."

Rachel sighed. "Now it's beginning to make sense. Somehow Lydia found out about the microchip and your sister's research. But what would Lydia do with research on repairing Darok domes?"

Gunter's expression suddenly turned serious. "Because what molecular robots can rebuild, they can also destroy."

Fear and anger swept over Rachel. "Oh my word! She's going to destroy the Daroks! We have to get out of here, Gunter! We have to stop Lydia from taking Micky's research to the United Quadrants! Are you telling me that the whole of First Quadrant could be destroyed all because Lydia Grant got hold of the microchip that you placed in box 15?"

"Nearly correct," said Gunter. "Lydia Grant *thinks* she's

got the microchip."

"Are you saying that she doesn't?" Rachel gasped.

Gunter's face crumpled. Just as Rachel thought he was about to cry, he let out an enormous guffaw. He laughed so hard that tears rolled down his cheeks. Rachel stared at him, baffled by the outburst.

He wiped the tears away. "I replaced the one I removed with a blank."

"So the chip Lydia has is useless?"

Gunter nodded. "The Daroks are safe."

Rachel's heart pounded with excitement. "But don't you see, Gunter? Lydia Grant will be back. When she realizes she has the wrong microchip, she'll come back looking for the real one! We'll persuade her to let us go in exchange for the real microchip. We'll get out of here."

"I doubt that'll happen," said Gunter, his expression taut and determined. "She'll be long gone—back to United Quadrants—before she discovers the truth."

"But she must have kidnapped you for a reason—you're probably her security in case anything went wrong. She'll be back."

Gunter shook his head. "I don't think Lydia *intended* to kidnap me. I must have stumbled on the open safe while she was still in the Cryolab. She probably realized that she couldn't let me tell anyone what I had discovered, and stuck me inside the safe because she didn't know where else to hide my body. I'm sure she had every intention of leaving me to die."

Rachel's heart sank. "So where *is* the real microchip?"

Gunter wagged his finger. "No more, Rachel. That's all I'm telling you—for your own good. If you don't know where it is, Lydia Grant can't threaten you and your family. I'll take the location of Micky's microchip to my grave."

* * * * *

Maddie bounded down the steps of the military jet and across the Darok 9 military hangar toward Will, who stood waiting with Commander Gillman and Major Wells.

"Will! I'm so glad you're okay!" She threw her arms around him and then drew back, embarrassed by her public display of affection. She felt her cheeks flush. Will's face had also colored noticeably.

"I was worried about you too," he said flashing his familiar wide grin. "From what Dad told Commander Gillman over the VisionCom, you've been busy since we got separated."

"I'll say."

"At least *you* got the information we went to Darok 10 for. Sorry I didn't make it."

"No worries. I just hope we can use it to find your mom and Mr. Havard...and maybe even Dr. Schumann."

Will's dad finally caught up with her. He hugged Will rigidly and muttered an apology about being a lousy father, then turned to salute Gillman.

"Did you find Uncle Hank?" asked Will.

"Sorry, son. We stormed Lazzar Technologies with a

special team as soon as we got word, but the building had been cleaned out. Not a trace of anyone or any equipment."

Maddie smiled. Captain Conroy talked to Will as if he were part of his military operation. She was glad her own father was more relaxed and approachable.

"As I thought," said Gillman, leading the party out of the hangar, down the stairs and into the back of the Darok 9 security force headquarters. "Chris, I assume you got clearance from James Manning to bring the file on Micky Rigby out of Darok 10?"

"That's what took the time in getting here. It's not easy to do anything with the amount of red tape at Quadrant HQ these days," Will's dad replied as they walked along the first floor corridor. He turned to scowl at Maddie walking behind and added, "Especially after Hank and Maddie broke into the records room. But yes, I've got it." He tapped his briefcase several times. "James realizes that this is a serious threat to the Daroks. As Quadrant Commander he has to do everything in his power to avert it."

"Maddie, have you heard anything from Havard since he called to you from the Galaxy Hotel?" asked Gillman.

"Not a thing," said Maddie, shaking her head.

"We must assume that Hank met up with Grant," said Captain Conroy. "He'll think Will is still a prisoner. I doubt that Grant would admit to him that Will had escaped."

"Agreed," said Gillman. "She'd want the extra leverage."

"Darok 10 security force is on full alert. I'm not worried about Hank." The Captain's voice was firm and determined. "They'll find him, and Grant and Lazzar as well."

"Good. We'll concentrate our efforts on locating your wife and Gunter Schumann. We'll start with Rigby's file," said Gillman, smiling for the first time since they arrived. He opened his office door and beckoned everyone inside.

Maddie's stomach knotted as she entered. She'd been in Gillman's office only once before—and on that occasion she'd broken in. Today, she took time to admire the expensive furnishings and the latest optical computer, which dominated the enormous desk.

Gillman pulled up extra chairs around a large oval table in the center of the room and everyone sat down.

Maddie could hardly believe she was being included. She sat next to Will at one end of the table, facing Commander Gillman, Major Wells and Captain Conroy.

There was a forceful knock on the door. A head of red hair was the first thing to appear around the frame.

"Ah, Mac! Come in and take a seat," said Gillman, rising to greet him. "Do you know everyone?"

"It's only the young lady I don't know," Mac replied, walking around to her end of the table.

"Madeleine Goren, meet Mac Stewart."

Mac tipped his head. "Pleased to meet you at last, young lady. Hank has told me great things about you."

Maddie smiled and shook his hand. She instantly liked the lanky man who treated her with such respect.

Gillman cleared his throat as if he had had enough of the pleasantries. "Good. We're all here. We'll start with Dr. Schumann. Let's see if we can piece together his known movements on Friday evening."

"I was the last person to see the doc," said Will. "He was acting very strange. He kept mopping his head with his handkerchief and I remember asking him if he was ill."

"What was his response?" asked Gillman.

"He said he was fine, but I got the feeling he was trying to get rid of me. The doc usually chats to me about cryonics, especially on a Friday night when he's packing up for the weekend."

"Where did you see him and at what time?" barked Captain Conroy in a tone as though his son were on trial.

"He was standing right in front of the Cryolab. It was just before I met Mom, so that'd be around six on Friday night."

"Okay," said Gillman, clearing his throat again. "That's now fifty-one hours ago. The Cryolab and Pathology Department have both been searched several times, but he could be elsewhere in the hospital. Schumann never signed out and was never seen leaving."

"My mom never signed out and wasn't seen leaving either," added Will.

"Number of hospital entrances?" asked Captain Conroy, almost as if he were organizing a military attack.

"There are two public entrances—the main one in the lobby and a side exit onto Canaveral Street," Gillman replied.

"Couldn't Schumann or Rachel have slipped out or been taken by Grant through the side exit?" asked Captain Conroy. "No sign-out is required there, correct?"

"Correct," replied Gillman. "But since the trouble with Lydia Grant last year an electronic security mechanism has been installed. Neither of them could have left the building without scanning their passes, *and* the time that they left would have been recorded on the main computer. We've interviewed all of the staff and no one resembling either Mrs. Conroy or Dr. Schumann has been seen leaving the building. We've even covered the possibility that they might have been carried out unconscious or wheeled out in a wheel chair."

"Then we must assume that they're both still in the hospital somewhere," said Conroy.

"Major Wells, I want you to deploy several security force sections to search this hospital thoroughly. They are to have access to every room and storage area," said Gillman.

"Understood, sir," said Wells, getting up and leaving.

Will's dad took over the discussion, pulling on his graying beard as he spoke in his formal military manner. "Summarizing, we know that Rigby was Schumann's sister and that she was frozen three years ago. Thanks to Maddie and Hank we know that Rigby's research could potentially be used to destroy the Daroks. That gives us Lydia's motive and it connects Schumann with this whole mess."

"I don't get why Lydia Grant thought she could get her

hands on the research when Micky Rigby is in tank 2 and all the files about her and her work are here with us," said Maddie.

"Very good point, Maddie. We're definitely missing something," agreed Gillman.

"What about the cryosafe?" asked Will.

Everyone turned to look at him.

Will stood up and leaned over the table. "Dr. Schumann once told me that every patient has a box in the cryosafe for their personal effects so that when they return to life on the Moon all their documents are ready for them."

"That's correct," said Gillman.

"Perhaps her research notes are in her box," suggested Maddie.

"Exactly what I was thinking," said Will. "I'll bet she recorded everything on memory cards."

Gillman thought for a moment. "They're small boxes, but memory cards could easily fit in them. Don't know why I didn't think of it."

"It would explain why Grant took Schumann in the first place," added Mac. "She would need his code to get into the cryosafe."

Gillman chuckled. "Not likely. We're talking about Lydia Grant—not your common thief. She'd easily hack the cryosafe code or know someone who could."

"That's why she was working with Randolph Lazzar," said Mac in a tone that suggested he had no doubt. "He's good at forensics and good with computer programs. Plus he's had security force clearance for eighteen months and could easily have hacked into the data base."

Maddie flushed, relieved that nobody had mentioned that she had hacked into the security force data base last year.

"Anyway, Mom's code wasn't exactly difficult to figure out," said Will. "Lydia Grant would have got it easily."

"Don't tell me," said Captain Conroy with a groan. "She didn't use SH33—Hank's wonder drug—again, did she?"

Will nodded. "'Fraid so, Dad."

Captain Conroy shook his head in disbelief.

"If Grant didn't need Schumann's help," Gillman continued, "then it's more likely that Schumann discovered what Grant was up to, so she had to shut him up."

"Which would explain why Dr. Schumann looked so worried when I saw him," said Will.

Commander Gillman pushed back his chair and rose. "It seems like a good suggestion, Will, and certainly the best solution yet. It still doesn't tell us where Gunter or Rachel are, but let's see if we can at least locate Micky Rigby's research in the cryosafe."

* * * * *

Rachel jumped to her feet. This time she *had* heard something—she was sure. It was a clicking noise, almost as if...was it possible? It sounded as though someone was opening the door to the cryosafe! She shot a hopeful glance at Gunter. "I knew they'd find us!"

"I didn't doubt it for a minute," he answered sarcastically, but there was no hiding his relief.

Rachel grabbed her bag and stood right in front of the door. Any moment now it would open and she'd be free. Her heart thumped madly. Who would she hug first? Will or Hank? Perhaps even Chris would be there to greet her.

The door began to open.

There stood her brother.

"Hank!" she cried with relief.

Tears rolled down her cheeks. "I knew you'd find us! It's been just awful in here! You can't imagine..." She stepped forward.

But Hank didn't move. He didn't speak—he didn't even smile. She'd never seen him like this. He remained steadfast, his expression stony, his mouth in a tight line. She could hear Gunter struggling to his feet behind her, groaning and breathing heavily.

"Hank? What's wrong?"

A familiar raucous laugh rang out from behind her brother. A shiver raced down Rachel's spine. She didn't need to see the face—she knew that laugh. Rachel instinctively stepped back into Gunter.

"Easy, Rachel," he whispered in her ear, supporting her arms. "Breathe deeply. Don't do anything rash."

Lydia Grant stepped out from behind Hank. Rachel saw her dark outline against the soft lighting from the

Cryolab. She was paralyzed with fear. When would this terrible ordeal end?

"Why is everyone so quiet?" Lydia asked, waving a laser in the air. "Nothing to say? Thought you'd looked death in the face and won, Mrs. Conroy? And Gunter, you're looking good...considering!"

"How did you get in here? How did you get past the guard in the foyer?" Rachel screamed.

"Where's your imagination, Mrs. Conroy? You don't think we just signed in at the front desk, do you?" Rachel tipped back her head and cackled. "There's always another way."

"But surely everyone's looking for us!"

"No one except Hank knows that you're missing, Mrs. Conroy. It's Sunday evening! Tomorrow, when you don't report for work, maybe then someone might notice."

"My husband and my son will have noticed—I didn't go home last night. They'll have a search party out by now!"

"Wrong again. I've got Will in Darok 10. I have your VisionCom and I picked up all of his messages to you. Decided to go for a little trip to visit his father, he did. What a shame..." She clucked. "He didn't quite get there! Your husband's too involved in looking for him at the moment to worry about you."

"What's...what's happened to Will?" stammered Rachel. "What have you done with him, you...you evil...you evil piece of work!" She rushed forward.

Lydia quickly pointed the laser at Hank's head. "Don't come any closer, or your brother dies." She glared at

Rachel with her penetrating cold black eyes.

"Hank, your face!" said Rachel, now close enough to see the huge gash across his cheek.

"Calm down, Rach," Hank muttered. "I'm okay and I'm sure Will is okay too."

"How touching, Hank!" snapped Lydia. "Especially since your meddling sister got you involved in the first place. But then, if it hadn't been for your insatiable curiosity and your desire to be a do-gooder, your nephew wouldn't be in trouble either, and I would have only had to deal with Schumann."

Rachel froze and stared at Hank, trying to understand what had just taken place, studying his face for a signal as to what she should do. Anything...a glint in his eye...a twitch...a nod? But his face was unreadable. He kept perfectly still. He said nothing to rile the woman—so unusual for Hank. He was never this calm. Did this mean he intended to cooperate with Lydia or did he have a plan?

"Move back inside!" Lydia hollered.

Shaken, Rachel inched backward, still searching for a sign from her brother.

Lydia shoved Hank into the cryosafe. "Stand next to your sister."

Hank steadied himself and lined up between Gunter and Rachel.

"That's better!" said Lydia. She tapped the laser against her cheek as if it were a toy. "Thought you'd outsmarted me, did you, doctor? Thought I wouldn't check the microchip before I left the Daroks? I made that mistake with Hank's precious SH33 and I wasn't about to make it again."

"I don't know what you mean," said Gunter. He stood tall and faced her, his mouth set in a defiant expression. "I have no idea what you're talking about. You hit me on the back of the head, and the next thing I know, I'm locked in the safe with my assistant. And you expect me to figure out what's going on in your twisted brain?"

Lydia's eyes flashed with outrage. "Well, Dr. Gunter Schumann, you're a stronger man than I thought, and either you think I'm a complete idiot, or you don't care what happens to the Conroy family." Her voice reached screaming pitch.

"What do you want?" Gunter demanded.

"Stop playing games, Dr. Schumann. You *know* what I want. I want the right microchip. The one *you* switched."

"I don't know about any microchip except the one that you've obviously already taken from box 15," said Gunter, showing no signs of bending.

Lydia glared at him, then tossed back her head and said coldly, "Now let's see...who does Gunter value most?"

Gunter stiffened as though she had struck him.

"Would it be the lovely Rachel, here? Or perhaps her clever, brilliant brother? Or maybe...yes, why not? Young Mr. Will Conroy." She pulled Rachel's VisionCom from her pocket with her left hand. "One Com call should take care of things. Should it be a broken leg or broken arm first?"

"Please, Lydia!" Rachel begged. A wave of nausea passed over her. How could she protect Will? She didn't even know where he was. "I'll do anything, but leave Will out of it."

"The words of a good mother," Lydia mocked. "Wasted on me, of course! What do I care about your snooping, self-absorbed brat?"

"Go on—make that call!" said Hank quietly.

Rachel turned and glared at her brother. "Hank, how could you? He's your nephew!"

"Go on, Lydia," Hank continued calmly, ignoring Rachel's rebuke. "I dare you to make that call! Why don't we think about this logically? You can't kill Gunter—he's got what you want. Kill him and the location of the microchip goes with him. You won't get rid of me—not yet. I'm too valuable to you. You need me just long enough to access the project code and download the research. What about my sister? No. You won't kill her in front of me and Gunter, because you know that if you do you'll *never* get what you want. You'll leave her here in the cryosafe as your security. There's no one here who's instantly expendable."

Lydia flipped open the Com. "Hank, despite your claim that you don't care about your nephew, I know you do. I've heard your passionate pleas on his behalf. Your supposed indifference to him will not change my mind!"

Rachel realized her mouth was gaping. What was

Hank trying to do?

"One last chance, Schumann," said Lydia. "Tell me where the microchip is or the boy *will* suffer."

Rachel gasped. "You wouldn't!" She bit down on her lip so hard that she tasted blood.

"Oh, but I would," snorted Lydia. "And how well you know that, Mrs. Conroy!"

Gunter stood firm. He looked at Rachel with eyes that begged forgiveness and then turned defiantly toward Lydia.

"Time's running out, Lydia," continued Hank, but with more aggression in his voice. "Your plan is falling apart. Chris Conroy will have organized search parties for all of us by now. As it is, you'll be lucky to get out of First Quadrant alive. You'd better make the call to scar-face or we'll know you haven't the stomach to pull this off." Hank took two steps forward. "Besides, Lazzar would do the deed—not you. He won't hurt my nephew."

"You think not, Hank?" said Lydia in a cool, calculating manner. "Are you willing to risk it, Schumann?" She raised the Com in front of her face.

Rachel swallowed the screams of anguish building at the back of her throat. What was Hank thinking?

Then Rachel understood.

Chapter 17

Hank's heart quickened. His opponent showed no signs of relenting—not that he had anticipated she would. He had prepared himself for this moment, carefully baiting her and patiently waiting. It was now or never. Could he succeed where he had failed the last time?

Lydia tossed back her head and laughed callously. Then she suddenly stiffened and regained her composure. "Time's up!" she snarled.

She gave a brutal stare, dialing the Com while keeping her eyes trained on the three of them. "What's going on?" she muttered. "Why won't this call go through?" She turned her gaze to the screen and dialed again.

In that brief second of distraction, Hank seized his opportunity. He ran at full speed through the open door of the safe and toward Lydia. She looked up with an expression of horror just as he flew at her.

Lydia spun around, dropping the Com but managing to steady the laser with both hands. "You idiot, Hank!" she spat, pointing the weapon at his forehead. "Now I see your game. You've sealed your fate and that of your precious family. The boy will die! Then we'll see if the doctor will cooperate or if the lovely Rachel will be next."

A cold knot formed in Hank's stomach. Was that the best he could do against such a formidable enemy? He'd had two attempts to knock her weapon away and failed on both occasions. Where was his ingenuity? His heart felt heavy. He felt weak and vulnerable for the first time. There was little he could do to stop her now.

"Please, Lydia..." begged Rachel.

"*Please*, Lydia? What kind of pathetic plea is that? The doctor had his chance and now Hank has just blown it for all of you. Get back in the safe with the others, Hank! I'll be back when I've made my call from ground level...where there *is* good reception!"

Gunter suddenly staggered forward. "Okay. Enough of this, Lydia. You win!" he said unsteadily. "If I cooperate and show you where I've hidden the *real* microchip, you will not harm the Conroy family and you will leave Darok 9 immediately after. Is that a deal?"

"Gunter, don't..." said Hank, swallowing hard. "Or thousands will die, not just us."

"Shut your mouth, Hank," snapped Lydia. "Or I'll shut it for you." She waved the laser in his direction. "The doctor is finally seeing sense, yet he has the audacity to try and cut a deal with me." An evil smile spread across her thin lips.

"Do you agree, woman?" said Gunter, with more force than Hank had ever heard him use before.

Lydia seemed taken aback. Her black eyes widened. She pushed her lips forward as if in thought and finally replied, "Deal. Where's the chip?"

"Stored safely in the Pathology Department."

Lydia's face brightened. "So close. Even better.

Okay, doctor. Move slowly forward out of the safe and close the door."

Rachel gasped as the heavy door shut again. Hank smiled bleakly at his sister in a weak attempt to offer reassurance, but inside he felt nothing but despair. Because he'd failed, he'd put the entire population of the Moon at risk. How could he have been so stupid?

* * * * *

Will's heart raced as they rode the elevator down to the basement. The anticipation of what they might find in the cryosafe was rising with every second. He stood in the back of the elevator with Maddie, the tall figures of Commander Gillman and Mac Stewart in front of them.

The elevator doors opened and Mac stepped out into the corridor.

"Lydia Grant!" Mac shouted. "She's got Schumann!" Then Mac fell to the floor, clutching his right arm and writhing in agony.

"Get down! Laser!" hollered Commander Gillman, in true army style.

"And as you can see, I'm not afraid to use it," Lydia shouted back. "Don't come an inch closer, Commander, or the doctor dies. I see that Mr. Stewart decided to accompany you."

Will lifted his head from the floor of the elevator to look at Lydia. As their eyes met, her mouth dropped in obvious shock.

"Well, well. If it isn't young Mr. Conroy," she said, the confusion evident in her voice.

"Mr. Lazzar's such a nice man," taunted Will, remaining flat on the floor. "He let me go. No decent human being would do what you've done. You're so evil that even your friends betray you."

"Shut it, brat!" Lydia hissed through clenched teeth. "One more word and I'll put Mr. Stewart out of his misery and finish him off permanently. Then we'll see how happy you are that Lazzar betrayed me!"

"No, please...don't do that!" screamed Will, horrified that his taunting had backfired. Mac was shaking with the shock and suffering quietly on the floor. Will stared into her black eyes across a ringing silence, silently praying that she wouldn't harm Uncle Hank's best friend. He felt like throwing up. He knew too well that Lydia Grant would kill Mac just for revenge.

Lydia's mouth was set in annoyance and her eyes dark and dangerous. "Mr. Conroy, if you value your friends' lives and you don't want a hole burned through your own brain, I suggest you don't open your mouth again."

Relief swept over him. He lowered his head to the floor and took a deep breath.

"The doctor and I are going to walk slowly backwards down this corridor and into the Pathology Department. Don't anyone move or the doctor dies. When I get what I came for, I just *might* let him go."

"*Please*, tell me what you've done with my Mom first!" shouted Will, lifting his head from the floor. He suddenly panicked at his outburst. What had he done? Lydia's sinister smile widened and thinned as she watched his discomfort and pain. Would she kill Mac as his punishment?

"She's locked in the cryosa—" Gunter blurted out, cut off in mid-sentence as Lydia hit him across the head with the laser.

"Stop trying to be smart, Schumann, or I'll finish off your friends right now!"

Gunter Schumann groaned and squeezed his eyelids as if trying to cope with the pain.

But the doc's words were enough for Will. His mom was alive and in the cryosafe—just down the hall. It was all he needed to know, for now. He could rescue her later. But first, what could he do to save the doc?

He watched Lydia and Gunter walk backward to the Pathology Department, the laser pointed at Gunter's head. If only there were another way down to the basement so that he could help the doc. Then in a flash, it came to him. *There is! There is another way!*

As Lydia and Gunter reached the swinging doors, Will scrambled to his feet and lunged for the elevator buttons. "Stay down!" he screamed at Maddie, and forced himself into the corner by the door, out of range of Lydia's weapon.

Lydia fired the laser through the closing elevator doors, penetrating the back wall.

"Don't move, Maddie!" shouted Will.

The laser fired again, erratically. Everything seemed to

be happening in slow motion. "Come on, close!" he shouted at the door.

The doors finally slid shut. Will sighed with relief. Maddie clambered off the floor as the elevator rose to the lobby. Her face was red with anger. "Thanks for saving *me*, Will, but what are you thinking? You've left Commander Gillman, Mackenzie Stewart and Dr. Schumann down there!"

"I finally get how she did it!" said Will excitedly. "I know how Lydia Grant got in and out of the hospital without being seen."

"So? How's that going to help?"

"Don't you see? We can cut off her escape route!"

Maddie's exasperated expression changed to one of admiration. "Tell me, quickly," she begged.

"There aren't two hospital entrances, there are three! When I came to collect Mom for dinner on Friday night she went out back to set the alarm on what she called the rear elevator."

"I've never seen it," said Maddie.

"It's not for the general public. The hospital uses the rear entrance to bring the dead down into the Pathology Department. After all, you can't exactly wheel them through the hospital lobby in full view of everyone."

"Great! But now you've worked out Grant's escape route, what are we going to do?"

"This time we call Darok 9 security force. No more playing hero for me."

"Good," said Maddie. "Wherever your Uncle Hank is

right now, I know he would agree with *that* decision!"

The bell sounded and the doors opened in the lobby.

"Let's go," said Will, tugging on Maddie's sleeve and racing to the desk in the lobby. "We've got to call Major Wells at security force headquarters. He's just got to get his men here in time!"

* * * * *

Hank thumped the floor hard. "Darn! I thought I could get to Lydia in time."

Rachel smiled sympathetically. "It was a brave effort, Hank."

"Thanks. Pity it wasn't good enough." He edged over to where his sister sat and put his arm around her. "I'm sorry that I got us into this mess. I'd never deliberately do anything to hurt you or Will. I hope you know that."

Rachel took his hand. "You may be bull-headed, stubborn and a lot of other things, but if there's one thing I know for sure, it's how much you love your family. Besides, didn't you say that it was me who got us into this mess?" she laughed.

"But then I persisted with the investigation and ignored your advice that we get the security force involved," replied Hank, ignoring his sister's attempt to be upbeat about their situation.

"What's done is done, Hank. We both will have to live with the outcome...or die with it."

"We'll get out of here," he shot back. "I promise."

"You can't promise, Hank. It's out of your hands this time." She picked up Gunter's music box from the floor, turned it over in her hands and sighed. "And to think I was so sure that this held the secret to the whole mystery."

"You're now convinced otherwise?"

Rachel nodded. "Just an old man's connection to his family. With his sister dead, it's all that Gunter has left."

"Beautifully carved, isn't it?"

"I can't believe I threatened to smash it if he didn't tell me about M.J. Rigby!"

"You did?"

Rachel chuckled. "I was so mad at him. It was all I could think of at the time. You should have seen Gunter's face. It was as if I had threatened to blow up the Moon! Come to think of it, his reaction was very different when he first found out I had the music box. He was nasty and actually quite frightening."

"Nasty? Frightening? You're talking about Gunter?"

"Uh-huh. Strange, I know. He's normally so placid. But he screamed at me. Told me I'd better forget I'd ever seen the box—that it was better that way. His reaction frightened me."

"It's strange that someone would say those things or get so worked up over a family heirloom." Hank took the music box from her.

"It seemed odd to me at the time. But then he made such a passionate plea and told me the tragic story of his sister, so I just dismissed it."

"Got the key?"

"It's over there on the floor."

Hank picked up the ribbon and watched the tiny key twirling on the end. "It still seems odd that Will found the key in Gunter's briefcase and it wasn't with the box. Why didn't Gunter keep the two things together if it's just a sentimental family heirloom?"

Rachel suddenly grabbed Hank's arm. "Now that we know that Gunter has hidden the real microchip, do you think he hid it in here? Could this thing have a false bottom?"

"But Rach, Gunter said the chip is in the Pathology Department."

"You don't *really* believe Gunter would hand it over to Lydia, do you? He told me he'd take the location of Micky's microchip to his grave."

Hank shrugged. He turned the music box upside down and pressed on the bottom. "Doesn't look like it has a false bottom." He put the key in the keyhole and turned it roughly.

"Careful, Hank! Sometimes you can over-wind old mechanical things."

"Don't worry. It won't go any further without forcing it." He lifted the lid and watched the ballerina rotate to the music. "Seems like a pretty normal music box to me."

"And you're *sure* there's no false bottom?" asked Rachel.

Hank shook his head. "Sorry, Rach. I think we're both trying to solve a mystery that doesn't exist. I think Gunter was telling the truth and he's going to give Lydia the real chip."

"You and I might survive if he does. But I know it's the wrong thing to wish for, because that would mean the whole lunar population will be at risk later on." She shook her head decisively. "No. Gunter won't give the chip to Lydia. He valued his sister's research. There's no way he'll pass over information that would help all humankind to someone like Lydia, who'd use it to destroy human life."

The music ended and the ballerina stopped turning.

"Let's try one last thing," said Rachel. "Try twisting the key in the opposite direction."

Hank sighed. "Give it up, Rach."

"Humor me, Hank and turn the key counter-clockwise. *Please*?"

"This is our last attempt. Then let's forget about the music box . . . okay?"

As he turned the key, there was a high-pitched click. The ballerina tipped forward on its base, revealing a small space.

Inside it lay a thin, black piece of plastic.

"Unbelievable!" said Hank, laughing as he pulled out the missing microchip. "You were right after all."

"I'm always right," said Rachel with a broad smile. "Don't you know that by now?"

"I gotta hand it to you...you've solved the mystery through your sheer persistence. Say, are you okay?" Hank asked, noticing that her face had turned suddenly white.

"Oh, Hank. Do you realize what this means?" she asked softly.

The amused look left Hank's eyes. He nodded. "Gunter's trying to save us all. He's bravely taken Lydia on a wild goose chase when he has no intention of giving her the real microchop."

"But she'll kill him when she finds out he's lying!"

Chapter 18

Will tore along the front of the hospital and rounded the corner of the building, Maddie at his side. Major Wells had said he was on his way with two security force sections and Will was praying that they would arrive in time.

As he raced down the alleyway he had a sudden sick feeling. What if he was wrong and Lydia had no intention of using the rear elevator to escape? He racked his brains trying to assure himself that he was right. There were several ground floor windows round the back of the hospital, but Lydia would have to go up in the other elevator from the basement and through the lobby to get to them. He could think of no other possible way that she could get out of the basement directly onto street level without being seen. This had to be her route.

"Over there on the wall!" pointed Maddie. "I think that's a security alarm panel."

"Yeah, I see the elevator doors."

"They're low to the ground, aren't they?" asked Maddie as she stopped and bent to examine the wide black doors. "The elevator must be less than three feet tall."

"That's because the bodies are wheeled in on a folded gurney and sent down. The elevator's so cramped inside that it's not one that the living would want to ride in."

"Unless you're Lydia Grant," added Maddie with a grin.

Will began to type in SH33 on the security alarm keypad. "I suspect that Mom used the same code for everything—she's not got a good memory for codes and passwords."

"Stop, Will!" shrieked Maddie, "We shouldn't attempt to go down to the basement. Lydia Grant will hear the elevator and she'll know someone is waiting for her. There's no telling what she'll do to Dr. Schumann if she thinks she can't escape."

Will stopped punching in numbers and quickly lowered his hand. He could feel the color rising in his cheeks. "Sorry, I wasn't thinking. So what *should* we do?"

"Wait for the security force, I guess. There's not much else we can do."

Will paced back and forth. He hated doing nothing.

Suddenly there was a continuous high-pitched mechanical squeal. He swung around and stared at the two doors. "It's the elevator! It's on its way up! Lydia must be coming!"

"What do we do to stop her from getting away?" asked Maddie. "The security force hasn't arrived."

"She's not escaping, if I have anything to do with it!" replied Will.

"But we don't have a weapon or any way to stop her. There's nothing here in the alleyway."

"We'll jump her!"

"What?" said Maddie, scowling. "You've got to be kidding! She's got a laser!"

"Get back against the wall to the left of the elevator doors. With any luck Lydia won't see us as she exits and we'll surprise her. It's two against one, after all."

Maddie said nothing, and Will wasn't sure if the look on her face was one of sheer incredulity at what they were about to attempt or pure fear.

A clunk sounded as the elevator reached the top of the shaft. Will pressed his back against the wall, his eyes focused on the two black doors. He swallowed hard. He just hoped that Lydia would exit to her left so she wouldn't see them.

His heart pounded as the doors opened. It was then that he realized they were in luck. Lydia was either lying flat on her back or crouched down in the small enclosure. She'd need several seconds to get out and stand upright.

The doors opened fully. A mop of red hair emerged and then two hands reached forward to the ground. Lydia had been crouching. Just as she moved her right leg out, Will saw his chance. He lunged from his hiding place, growling loudly like some beast attacking its prey. He swept his foot across her right ankle and knocked her off balance.

Lydia screamed and fell onto her side, sprawled across the alleyway. She groaned, as if hurt by her fall, but immediately reached for the weapon tucked in her belt.

"She's going for her laser!" Maddie hollered.

Will pounced on top of Lydia, pushing her onto her back and forcing her arms above her head.

"Get off me, you brat!" she screamed, kicking and writhing beneath his weight.

"Grab the laser!" Will shouted to Maddie. While Maddie fumbled for the weapon, he held Lydia's wrists tightly and looked into the dark magnetic centers of her eyes. Sheer loathing welled within him. He didn't know it was possible to feel such deep hatred for another human being. But this wasn't just anyone. This was Lydia Grant, who had tried to destroy his family more than once, who had no regard for human life, and who was prepared to do anything to get what she wanted, no matter how much pain it caused.

"I've got the laser, Will," said Maddie, relief in her voice. "And it's pointed at your head, Lydia Grant!"

"So what!" she snapped. "You don't have the guts to use it, you dumb girl!"

"Don't try me," said Maddie.

"Idle threats," said Lydia as she continued to struggle. Will's arms grew weak. She was much stronger than he had expected, considering her small build. He was losing his grip on her wrists. How long could he hold her to the ground? Where was the security force? He wouldn't let this woman escape. He stared at her, hoping that she could read the hatred in his eyes.

"I said get off me!" she spat, clenching her teeth and snarling like a caged animal.

With a huge shove Lydia pushed him over and Will rolled to the ground. He scrambled to his feet but she was already up and lunging at Maddie.

Maddie's eyes were wide with fear. Both hands gripped the laser aimed at Lydia, but her arms shook violently.

Will held his breath, paralyzed. His heart pounded against his chest. He wanted to shout, "Shoot her, Maddie!" but the words wouldn't leave his lips.

It was as if time stood still.

Lydia Grant screamed and then screamed again. She fell to the ground clutching her side, contorted in agony.

Will looked at Maddie in disbelief. She had fired the laser. Her arms still shook and her eyes were glazed over. They had both underestimated Maddie's strength of character.

"Are you all right?" asked Will, prying the gun from Maddie's fingers.

"I...I...think so. I didn't want to kill her," said Maddie. "Just didn't know what else to do."

"It's okay, Maddie—she's injured, not dead. You did what you had to—what anyone would have done. You stopped her."

"Will! Maddie!" shouted Major Wells. He jogged down the alley toward them with at least twenty security force officers close behind. "Great going! We'll take over now."

Surrounded by officers, their weapons ready, Major Wells arrested Lydia Grant and read her the First Quadrant Code of Rights.

The Darok 9 ambulance, sirens wailing, backed into the alley. Michael One and Michael Two lifted Lydia onto a stretcher. Her expression was stony as they cuffed her to the stretcher rails.

"Brat!" she spat at Will. "You think this is over? Well, think again! *This* is just the beginning."

Will watched the Michael section carry her to the ambulance. Lydia lifted her head and gave him a piercing stare.

"You'll never sleep easy, Will Conroy!" she shouted from the ambulance. "I'll be back—and next time I'll kill you without a thought!"

Major Wells laughed. "Don't listen to a word of that nonsense. Locked in the First Quadrant Prison, hundreds of miles from any of the Daroks, she'll not be going anywhere for the rest of her days."

Maddie bowed her head and muttered, "I hope she's really gone for good, Will."

"It's just threats," said Will, shrugging it off. He drew in a deep breath and realized that he was shaking. Deep down he wondered how long it would take to put this all behind him.

"You both okay?" asked Major Wells.

"We're fine, thanks," said Will, getting a nod from Maddie.

"How are Commander Gillman and Mackenzie Stewart?" Maddie asked.

"The Commander wasn't hurt and Mac is being treated in hospital. He'll be okay in a day or two. Unfortunately . . . I'm sorry...but I wish I could say the same for Gunter Schumann."

Will felt suddenly hot. "What do you mean? What's

happened to the doc?"

"I'm sorry, Will. The Commander has just informed me that Gunter didn't make it. Lydia grant shot him. He was a very brave man."

Will couldn't hold back his tears. His heart felt heavy and the overwhelming sadness that enveloped him was almost more than he could bear. "Not the doc. Please, not the doc. He was the only one who really understood."

Maddie grabbed his hand. "Understood what?"

"Why I loved the Cryolab," he mumbled, wiping his face on his sleeve. "He always had time for me. Always explained everything about the current cryonics research. I swear, if it's the last thing I do, I'll find a way to bring Micky Rigby back to life and prove that the time he spent with me wasn't for nothing. I'm going to be the best cryonics scientist the Moon has ever seen."

"I'm sure you will," said Major Wells. "You're a bright and determined young man. I'm sure that Gunter was proud to be your mentor."

"Come on, Will," said Maddie, grabbing his hand. "We'll help each other through this. Let's go and see if they've got your mom out of the cryosafe. I'm sure she'll be really happy to see you."

Will dried his eyes and managed a smile. "Yeah. I'll be really happy to see her too. Now we just have to find Uncle Hank."

* * * * *

Will reached the door to the Cryolab just as the Commander was instructing the Henry section to open the safe. His father was already there, an anxious look set on his face.

Will walked up to his dad still teary eyed.

"I'm sorry about Gunter," said his dad. "I know he was a like a grandfather to you." He put his arm tenderly around Will's shoulder.

Will moved in closer and wrapped his arm around his father's waist. It had been a long time since he had really hugged his father. "Thanks, Dad. He was a good friend," he muttered. "I'll miss him terribly. Friday nights will never be the same again."

"Let's just hope your mother is okay."

"I'm praying hard," said Will. He'd already lost Gunter Schumann. If his mother had been hurt as well, he didn't know how he would cope.

Henry One and Henry Two heaved open the door.

Will's heart quickened. Then, in the dim light, he saw his mother, with her delicate features and dark hair. She looked drawn and tired, but she was very much alive.

"Will! Chris! Thank goodness!" She ran up to them and embraced them both tightly, tears running down her cheeks.

"Hank!" said Commander Gillman, surprise in his voice. "We thought you were in Darok 10!"

"I was," he replied. "It's a long story."

Will untangled himself from his mother's arms and ran to greet his uncle. "I'm so glad you're okay. Losing the doc was bad enough, but if I'd lost you or Mom..."

"What?" gasped Rachel, turning to look at him. "What do you mean, *losing* Dr. Schumann?"

Will gulped. "Sorry, Mom. I didn't mean for you to find out like this. I was going to tell you later. Lydia killed Dr. Schumann."

Rachel's lips quivered. "Oh, Gunter. You brave, dear man." Her face crumpled and she put her head in her hands and sobbed quietly.

"At least Lydia didn't get what she wanted and the Daroks are safe for now," said Hank. He held out the microchip and dropped it into Gillman's open hand. "This is what it was all about, Commander. Micky Rigby's research. Had Lydia managed to get this to United Quadrant scientists we would have had a lunar war."

Gillman looked shocked. "There's obviously a lot I don't know. I think you had better fill in the gaps for us. Take tonight to celebrate with your family and we'll meet at ten tomorrow morning in my office."

"What about Randolph Lazzar?" asked Will, suddenly remembering his heart-stopping escape from Darok 10.

Gillman shook his head. "Sorry. The Darok 10 security force hasn't found him. It seems that he's our one loose end in this whole mess. But at least he didn't take any valuable information with him. I'm sure he's long gone and he won't dare show his face again in the Daroks."

Will decided not to say anything, but had a feeling that he hadn't seen the last of Randolph Lazzar. He caught his uncle's glance. Judging by Hank's expression, Will guessed he was thinking the same thing.

"Okay, let's all get out of here," said his dad. "I'm sure Rachel and Hank can't wait to get home."

Will followed his parents to the door. He took one last look at the enormous cryotanks. "Someday, Micky Rigby," he said. "Someday I'll set you free."

H. J. Ralles

H.J. Ralles lives in a Dallas suburb with her husband,
two teenage sons, and a devoted black Labrador.
Darok 10 is her fifth novel.

Visit H. J. Ralles at her website

http://www.hjralles.com

Also By H.J. Ralles

Darok 9 ISBN # 1-929976-10-0 Top Publications

January 2002In 2120AD, the barren surface of the moon is the only home that three generations of earth's survivors have ever known. Towns, called Daroks, protect inhabitants from the extreme lunar temperatures. But life is harsh. Hank Havard, a young scientist is secretly perfecting SH33, a drug that eliminates the body's need for water. When his First Quadrant laboratory is attacked, Hank saves his research onto memory card and runs from the enemy. Aided by Will, his teenage nephew, and Maddie, Will's computer-literate classmate, Hank must conceal SH33 from the dreaded Fourth Quadrant. But suddenly Will's life is in danger. Who can Hank trust - and is the enemy really closer to home?

The Keeper Series

Keeper of the Kingdom Book I

ISBN # 1-929976-03-8 Top Publications
January 2001

In 2540AD, the Kingdom of Zaul is an inhospitable world controlled by Cybergon 'Protectors' and ruled by 'The Keeper'. Humans are 'Worker' slaves, eliminated without thought. Thank goodness this is just a computer game – or is it? For Matt, the Kingdom of Zaul becomes all too real when his computer jams and he is sucked into the game. Now he is trapped, hunted by the Protectors and hiding among the Workers to survive. Matt must use his knowledge of computers and technology to free the people of Zaul and return to his own world. Keeper of the Kingdom is a gripping tale of technology out of control.

Keeper of the Realm Book II

ISBN# 1-929976-21-6 Top Publications
January 2003

Matt is trapped in his computer game! Three hundred feet below sea level he faces his second terrifying mission. The tyrannical Noxerans have invaded the beautiful Realm of Karn. Matt's laptop is locked in the Noxeran Vault and the penalty for crossing into enemy territory is death! With the help of his friends, Varl and Targon, and Keela, the mysterious girl from Karn, he sets off on a frightening underwater expedition. But his plan goes dreadfully wrong. Winning level two of his game, without destroying the entire Realm, looks to be an impossible task.

Keeper of the Empire
Book III

ISBN# 1-929976-25-9 Top Publications
January 2004

The Vorgs have landed! They're grotesque, they spit venom and Matt is about to be their next victim. What are these lizard-like creatures doing in Gova? Why are humans wandering around like zombies? In the third book of the Keeper series, Matt finds himself in a terrifying world. With the help of his friend Targon, and a daring girl named Angel, Matt must locate the secret hideout of the Govan Resistance. And what has become of the wise old scientist, Varl? There is no end to the action and excitement as Matt attempts to track down the Keeper, and win the next level of his computer game.

The Keeper Series Continues . . .

Keeper of the Colony - Book IV

Beware! When the curfew bell tolls in the Dark End you had better be off the street! The icy Colony of Javeer, brutally ruled by Horando and his Gulden Guard, is a horrific setting for Level 4 of Matt's computer game. Targon has disappeared and Varl has been arrested and thrown into Central Jail. When Matt attempts to rescue Varl with the help of his new friends, Keir and Bronya Logan, he learns that Horando is not the only enemy he must beat. Gnashers live deep in the gold mines and are killing humans that dare to enter. But Horando will stop at nothing when it comes to increasing his stock of gold—even if it means sending thousands of humans to their death. Can Matt defeat Horando and save Varl before he becomes the next victim of the Gnashers?